JULIE ELIZABETH LETO
The Domino Effect

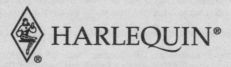

HARLEQUIN®

TORONTO • NEW YORK • LONDON
AMSTERDAM • PARIS • SYDNEY • HAMBURG
STOCKHOLM • ATHENS • TOKYO • MILAN • MADRID
PRAGUE • WARSAW • BUDAPEST • AUCKLAND

ISBN-13: 978-0-373-79276-4
ISBN-10:   0-373-79276-X

THE DOMINO EFFECT

Luke placed the blindfold over her eyes

"Are you sure you should trust me like this? We don't know each other."

Domino licked her lips, knowing he was watching. "That's part of the thrill. Just what is this dangerous man going to do to me?"

He'd stepped away. The air stilled. She couldn't even hear him breathing. What would he do next? This sexy, unassuming nightclub owner who might just be in league with international terrorists hell-bent on destroying the world?

When his lips crashed against her neck, she nearly leaped out of her skin. His teeth rasped against her flesh, reminding her that the sensation could easily have been a knife.

He slid his hand over her shoulder and cupped her breasts. "Whoa. What tensed you up so fast?"

She swallowed. "You surprised me."

"Isn't that what you wanted?" He wrapped his lips around her hardened nipple.

Her heartbeat accelerated and her breath shortened. "Yes," she said.

"Well, you haven't seen anything yet...."

Blaze™

Dear Reader,

I like to take chances. No, I don't jump out of airplanes or kayak down white-water rapids, but when I create a novel, I like to push limits. I like to create characters who aren't easily defined, and more and more lately, I'm exploring the good girl/bad girl dichotomy in my heroines.

Domino Black is perhaps my edgiest heroine to date—even more so than my oversexed romance writer in *Brazen & Burning* or my former heroin addict in *Up to No Good*. When I told my editor about Domino's profession, she instantly placed the book under the EXTREME BLAZE banner. As you read, you'll find out why. I also paired her with a deliciously sexy hero in Luke Brasco, so within the web of intrigue of *The Domino Effect,* I promise you'll find a real love story between people who couldn't be more different and yet share the same heart, even when the stakes are life and death.

And for all my readers who like to find character connections between my books (see my Web site at www.julieleto.com for more on that!) you may have a field day with this one. Let me know what you think by writing me at julie@julieleto.com. I'd love to hear from you!

Happy reading!

Julie Elizabeth Leto

A NOTE FROM JULIE

This past May, Harlequin rereleased two of my 2001 Harlequin Temptation titles (*Pure Chance* and *Insatiable*) in the *New Orleans Nights* collection. On the cover there was a flash that said, "Help Rebuild New Orleans... see inside," but a letter that explained how buying the book would benefit the charity Renew New Orleans (www.renewNOLA.org) was inadvertently left out. If you are interested in helping this amazing city rebuild—and in enjoying two of my books and a short story (never before in print) set in the French Quarter, Garden and Business districts pre-Katrina, please visit my Web site (www.julieleto.com) or your favorite online bookseller. Fifty percent of my personal proceeds from the sale of this book will benefit Renew New Orleans, a grassroots effort to help those in need.

Thank you and *laissez les bons temps rouler!*

Books by Julie Elizabeth Leto

For all the people around me—my editor, my agent, my family, my friends and neighbors and acquaintances—who seem to have no problem with the fact that I talk about my characters as if they are real. To me, they are. To my readers, they are. So thanks for not thinking I'm crazy—or if you do think I'm crazy, for not saying so to my face.

1

WITH A QUIET CLICK, Luke Brasco shut the door to the security room three floors above Club Cicero, Chicago's hottest night spot west of the famed Magnificent Mile. Mikey Maldonado, Luke's chief bouncer, swiveled from the bank of monitors he'd been watching and gave his boss a toothy grin.

"What's up, boss?"

Luke's gaze darted to the central screen. She was there. Dead center on the dance floor, commanding a tight and controlled space that no other man or woman dared invade. He'd noticed her seconds after she'd entered the club twenty minutes ago and, despite his best efforts, had been watching her exclusively ever since. Five minutes in, she'd eased by him at the bar, sparing him no more than a cursory glance. But her blue eyes—faceted and hypnotic—had yanked him instantly into her universe.

At first, he'd come upstairs to escape her allure. Now, he had different ideas.

Luke cleared his throat. "We've got a rowdy crowd out front," Luke explained.

Tucked under Michigan Avenue and Grand, only a

block from the famed Billy Goat Tavern, the gangster-themed nightclub, named for the area of Chicago where Capone made his fortune, was the ultimate speakeasy fantasy. Club Cicero brought in a range of customers from international businessmen wanting a taste of old Chicago to hip, urban partiers looking for a reason to wear fedoras and glittery, bugle-beaded dresses. Not that everyone dipped into roaring twenties fashion trunks before hitting the line that snaked around the building, but those that did created an atmosphere that made Club Cicero the place to be, and thus earned them a better chance at getting in.

His mystery woman hadn't needed a gimmick to cut to the front of the line. Her looks reflected an exotic background—almond-shaped eyes, olive skin, generous lips. She was neither petite nor tall—but she was anything but average. In skintight, hip-hugging charcoal jeans, a filmy black, stomach-baring tank top, a cropped leather jacket and impossibly high-heeled boots, she was every bit the woman he'd cook up in his fantasies when his bed seemed particularly cold or empty. And yet, Luke couldn't shake the feeling that, like the women in flapper hats and fishnet stockings, she was playing dress-up.

Just for him.

"Why don't you go down and give Craig a hand at the door?" Luke suggested. "I'll watch the cameras."

Mikey arched a brow, but pushed away from the desk nonetheless. Luke had made an odd request, but he was the boss and no one, with the exception of his stepmother, ever questioned his authority. He'd been running a bar in this location for nearly ten years now and no matter what the name or theme, he rarely took over for his surveillance guys unless someone had called in sick.

But not tonight. At this moment, he wanted to be alone to keep an eye on the five-foot-seven-inch package of pure living and breathing feminine power that had squeezed through the crowd near the bar. She'd tantalized him with a bold, spicy scent that somehow overpowered the hot sweat and free-flowing alcohol sizzling through the club. He'd been a bar owner for so long, he'd thought himself immune to such blatant sexuality. He *had* been immune.

Until her.

He realized then that Mikey had left and closed the door behind him, leaving Luke alone in the cramped surveillance room. He'd added the high-tech gadgetry two years ago after a local police investigation revealed that drugs were being sold in his club, patron to patron. At the time, he'd thought the Brasco family curse had once again caught up with him, that like his mafia-connected (and murdered) grandfather, his no-good, deadbeat absentee father and his convict half brother, he'd be doomed to failure. He'd called in every financial favor he'd ever had to buy the cameras and digital recording devices to keep away the riffraff. And he'd upped the cover charge to not only recoup his losses, but to demand a higher class of clientele. So far, his strategy had kept crime out of the club. But he'd never imagined he'd use the equipment to spy on a woman.

Luke slid into the cracked leather chair, still warm

from Mikey's two-hundred-fifty-pound bulk. He shifted, glanced down at the keyboard in front of him and tried to remember how to work the controls. As he fiddled, he glanced up at his mystery woman, determined not to lose sight of her.

The music changed. Slowed. What had been frenetic and quick now turned soulful and hot. He watched her face as she switched gears, at the tiny smile that danced across her generous lips. Her confidence never wavered. She could dance no matter the rhythm, but this way— purposeful, deliberate, intense—she obviously liked best.

This was insane. Desperate and pathetic, even. Luke had dated off and on since his broken engagement— yet another indicator that his genetic makeup doomed him—but he'd always been careful in his selections. He'd played it safe. No blue-eyed brunettes. No sleek, sexy creatures with inherent rhythm in their movements or throaty laughs that sent chills up his spine. No ladies—blond, brunette or redhead—with tattoos.

And no one, absolutely no one, who wanted more than a one-night stand.

But, man, one look at this chick in black and he rethought his strategy. A woman like her might not be fully enjoyed in a few hours' time. A woman like her might take at least a week or so to savor.

God, he had it bad.

Finally locating the tiny joystick on the edge of the control panel, Luke manipulated the image on the screen until he'd zoomed in on her. The security cameras, in vivid yet slightly grainy color, emphasized how she'd immersed herself completely in the music, a sensual dance-club tune with equal parts provocative lyrics to incendiary background moaning. The entire dance floor writhed with bodies simulating sexual pleasure—shoulders rolling, hips swinging, pressing torsos in full contact—until nothing kept them from doing the deed on the dance floor except the clothes they wore. And yet, Luke's mystery woman remained front and center, even though she danced alone.

Luke pushed back on the wheeled chair, stood and headed toward the door. Clearly he'd lost his mind. She wasn't anything special. She was probably just some oversexed chick shopping the prime cuts, looking for some hot body to pick up, take home and screw all night without asking his name.

He'd seen the type a thousand times.

Of course, he preferred women without expectations—women who wanted no semblance of a relationship that might threaten his carefully ordered life. He'd learned his lesson with Cecily, his ex-fiancée. He'd let her in and look how that had turned out.

But this one…

Luke returned to the control station.

"Who are you?" he asked the image on the screen. "And why can't I take my eyes off you?"

Her gaze flashed up at the camera, as if she'd heard, as if she could stare right through the lens straight into his eyes. Her lashes dropped to half-mast and her mouth curved into a smile that promised more than any man could possibly resist.

From below, the music pounded. The bass beat

thrummed off the soundproof walls, vibrated through the steel girders and injected directly into Luke's bloodstream. With slowness borne out of keen precision, she lifted her arms, taking her time, inching her hands up her thighs, across her hips, over her slim belly where she flicked the tiny ring of gold glittering at her navel.

Luke's midsection tensed and then the tightness quickly shot downward. He shifted in his seat, and after a glance toward the door, decided that fighting the inevitable wasn't worth the effort.

He surrendered, transfixed, enraptured, unable to remember the last time he'd indulged in something so wicked, so indulgent, as watching this woman dance. She eased her touch up her rib cage, splayed her palms over her breasts, then stroked higher, up her neck until she speared the fingers of one hand through her hair and allowed the other one to drift down her face so that her diamond-accented pinkie smeared the glossy red color she wore on her lips.

The distinct shade that would leave evidence on a certain body part.

Only when his lungs ached did Luke realize he wasn't breathing. The pace of the song picked up and she responded, slashing her hair across her face. She turned to some guy who'd invaded her space. She didn't hesitate for an instant, but pressed her body boldly against him.

The interloper instantly grabbed her hips.

Luke stood.

The jerk clutched her ass.

Luke shot out the door.

By the time he raced down two flights of stairs and burst through the crowd, he found the offender—knees on the dance floor, eyes red and watery—clutching his groin.

Luke grinned. He liked this girl.

But when he looked up and around, he couldn't find her.

He pushed toward the bar.

"Gloria!" he commanded.

His stepmother sauntered over, shouting out the punch line to one of her signature dirty jokes as she moved. The end of the bar where she'd been holding court erupted in laughter, bringing a naughty twinkle to her inscrutable onyx eyes.

"Whatcha need, Luke?"

"Did you see the girl on the dance floor? Black hair? Black tank top? Leather jacket? Tight jeans and roach killer boots?"

"You just described twenty percent of your female patrons."

Luke glanced around. How wrong his stepmother was. "This one you would have noticed."

Gloria shrugged and patted her perfectly coiffed, blond-streaked hair. "They're all a dime a dozen," she said, leaning across the bar so as to not insult any of the paying customers.

"No. She's different."

Gloria arched a brow and Luke realized his mistake. Since his father had married the former Broadway dancer when Luke had been six years old, Gloria D'Angelino Brasco had never acted much like a stepmother, except, perhaps, in the Cinderella sense. Sure, she'd given him lunch money when he reminded her and she'd made sure he left the apartment in time to meet his school bus, but otherwise, Gloria's interests in Luke and his half brother, Marcus, had remained cursory until they'd grown into men. Once they could drink together, cuss together and watch R-rated movies together, they'd all become buddies. When he'd opened his first club at this location over ten years ago, she'd fronted him some of the money from the stash his father had left after his disappearance. She'd also worked the hostess stand, waited tables and eventually, ended up behind the bar. What she rarely did was get involved in his love life—at least, not in a positive way. In her estimation, no woman was good enough for him or her biological son, Marcus, whose love life wasn't anyone's concern now that he was doing time in federal prison.

But because of the interest Luke had just shown, Gloria would now hate the mystery woman on sight.

"Never mind," he said, then pointed toward a college kid waving a twenty in her direction.

Gloria instantly responded. She'd likely sell the guy a pair of six-dollar Zombies and finagle the rest as a tip.

Unable to let his woman-in-black escape so easily, Luke weaved his way through the crowd, searching for a flash of blue-black hair, but by the time he realized how much he was acting like some pathetic loser, he also realized she was gone.

They had a capacity crowd, yet the place seemed empty.

He dashed outside. When the horde lined up in the roped area against the brick wall realized his exit didn't mean someone else could enter, a collective groan rent the air, battling with the music still pulsing from inside.

"Something wrong, boss?"

Mikey nudged Craig. Between the two of them, they could take on the entire defensive line of the Bears—and win. Luke watched his bouncers inflate at the suggestion of trouble, but he waved them off. He didn't need everyone at Club Cicero thinking he'd gone nuts.

He jogged to the edge of the sidewalk. The street, as usual, was quiet at this time of night. One block over, however, Michigan overflowed with cars and taxis and even horse-drawn carriages for the tourists. Traffic and headlights dulled his ability to see. She was gone.

Perhaps that wasn't such a bad thing.

He cursed his overactive libido and returned to the club.

"You sure everything's okay?" Mikey asked, his mouth skewed in an expression that Luke definitely wouldn't want to see in a dark alley. His chief bouncer, a former National Guardsman with tours of duty in Iraq and Afghanistan under his belt, invoked fear with no more than a sneer.

Luke shook his head and blew out a relieved breath. "Nothing's wrong. In fact, I think fate just did me a favor."

"YOU FAILED TO MAKE CONTACT."

Domino Black speared her hand through her sweaty, ironed-straight hair, leaned back in the cab seat and casually whispered into the clasp of her Agency-issued watchband. "That's a matter of opinion."

The reception of her invisible earpiece had been fine-tuned, designed for crystal-clear reception even in a noisy nightspot like Club Cicero. The Agency had patched into Club Cicero's surveillance system and her one and only handler, the enigmatic and perennially arrogant Darwin, had given her a play-by-play of Brasco's movements the entire time she'd been at the club. That's how she knew her plan had worked. That's how she knew that after two weeks of paying the exorbitant cover charge to enter the club, each time in a different disguise, she'd finally found the combination of hair, makeup, clothes and eye color that floated Luke Brasco's boat. Funny how he'd chosen the incarnation that was closest to her normal look. She would have saved herself a lot of trouble if she'd tried going natural the first time.

"I saw no direct interaction," Darwin retorted.

"Sometimes the indirect can be even more powerful," she whispered, glancing at the taxi driver. Not that she gave a damn if the guy thought she was some wacko for talking to herself, but she trusted no one. For all she knew, the guy was a counterspy sent to disrupt her current operation. The weight of her gun on her ankle pushed the thought away. If he was, he'd be dead before he could make her so much as stub her toe.

"Explain," Darwin ordered.

"I don't think I should," she teased. "I seem to remember a memo prohibiting the sharing of pornographic material over secure Agency frequencies."

Darwin sighed, a rare sign of frustration from her notoriously cool and collected handler.

"Report to the rendezvous. Darwin out."

Triumphant, Domino plucked the listening device from her ear and stuffed it into her bra, then relaxed into the vinyl seat of the cab, not caring that the soles of her boots were sticking to the grimy cab floor. She'd been in more disgusting places than this car on too many occasions to count. In fact, as far as assignments went, this one was ice cream compared to her usual jobs.

When the cabbie made a wrong turn on La Salle, she shouted at him in Farsi not to jerk her around, then cursed in English about the way taxi drivers thought they could screw around with female fares. Not that Domino knew much about Chicago, but as an operative for The Shadow, a black ops unit currently associated with a Homeland Security task force, Domino had been trained to speak, act and respond like any native of the Windy City. She knew the hotspots, the tourist traps and the best place to get an Italian steak sandwich. She could disappear into the sewers beneath Cabrini Green and come out a block from the Sears Tower. She'd studied the train tunnels and elevated platforms. She knew the location of every police station within a thirty-mile radius of the city center.

She doubted any of this knowledge would be needed in her current assignment—this job seemed oddly vague—but she'd never questioned the judgment of the briefing team. And she never doubted her orders or the veracity of her handler. Since her recruitment at fifteen years old, she'd worked exclusively with

Darwin and, to date, he'd never steered her wrong, even if she didn't know his last name, where he'd been born, what he did in his spare time or even if he had a life beyond The Shadow, which she doubted.

She had no life, so why should he?

The taxi pulled up to a light and Domino checked the cross streets to make sure the driver wasn't screwing with her again. Confident he'd learned his lesson, she gave herself a moment to think about how this assignment differed from her normal operation— go in, eliminate whatever threat had been targeted, then disappear. Odd thing was, Lucas Brasco had yet to be identified as a target. He was, in the manner of politically correct double-speak, a "person of interest."

Domino closed her eyes, imagining for a decadent moment how the situation tonight might have changed had she allowed Luke Brasco to join her on the dance floor. Would he have groped her like the asshole she'd chosen simply to stoke Brasco's fire, or would he have possessed more finesse? The fact that he'd retreated upstairs to watch from the surveillance camera intrigued her. She'd attended a briefing regarding the man's private life. He'd had his share of lovers. By all reports, he was outgoing and popular. He'd banked on his people skills to build a business that made just about every club owner in Chicago envious.

So why had he watched her from afar?

She peeked one eye open and checked the driver in the rearview as he accelerated forward. A second later, she witnessed a flash of wide-eyed surprise in his eyes. Then, a smash from behind.

Domino flew forward. She blocked the impact against the Plexiglas with her arms. The taxi skidded to a stop, jumped a curb and smashed into a light pole. Domino rolled with the movement, slipping into survival mode. Once they were still, she slid out of the car door opposite the driver's side, gun in hand.

"Oh, my God! Are you all right?"

Bystander.

She palmed her weapon and pasted on a friendly grin. Out of the corner of her eye, she spied the cab-driver stagger out of the smashed car and advance on the offending tailgater who'd rammed his bumper into their back end. She instantly noted make, model, color and driver description.

His engine was still running. No air bags deployed. She saw his tires turn toward the road.

The bastard was going to run.

The cabdriver pounded on the driver's window, shouting some rather choice insults, some of the best she'd heard since the last time she was in Tehran. The other driver was about to take off. Domino waved away the help that had started to gather near her and slipped through the guy's unlocked passenger door, closing and locking it behind her.

"What the hell do you think you're doing?" the driver slurred.

Drunk. Nice.

Or acting drunk to cover a hit.

"I could ask you the same thing."

She leaned forward, her weapon aimed subtly at the man's heart. He didn't even notice. One inhalation and she was nearly knocked off balance by the whiskey reeking through his pores. At the red, dilated eyes that could barely focus and the bottle on the floorboard, Domino guessed this one wasn't going to be much trouble.

"Hosting a mobile happy hour, are you?"

"Wha?"

In her line of work, Domino rarely had time for banter. And clearly, this dude wasn't up to the task.

"I'm getting the hell out of here," the driver shouted.

Grinding axles shook the car. The taxi driver increased his assault on the window, pounding as he climbed onto the hood. Domino, however, slid her hand across the top of the seat, easing her fingers into the man's sweaty, greasy hair.

"So soon? We were just starting to get to know one another."

She didn't give him a chance to reply. One skilled pinch to the carotid artery and he fell forward, his head banging the steering wheel.

Domino patted him on the shoulder and removed the keys from the ignition. "That's going to hurt like hell in the morning, you candy-assed son of a bitch."

She popped the lock on the driver's side door, then eased out on the passenger side. The taxi driver stared at her as if she'd sprung a second head. She winked at him and tossed him the keys.

"I'll assume my fare is on the house?"

He looked at her oddly. She didn't bother to translate. Sirens wailed from the next block over. The crowd swelled. Domino faded into the shadows just as the cops pulled up at the scene. Mildly curious, she stuck around, amused by the kaleidoscope of blue and red swirling around her. She listened to the investigators as they spilled onto the scene and smiled when even the bystanders who'd watched her every move since she'd exited the taxi disagreed about what she looked like and where she'd gone.

If tonight was an omen, this job was going to be a piece of cake. In, out, done. No regrets. No excitement. Except, maybe, the sexual kind.

2

AFTER THE ACCIDENT, the trip to the rendezvous point was relatively uneventful. Domino concentrated on reaching the safe house quickly and without being seen. Reminded her of her early training. Fifteen years old. Father dead, mother locked up. A loner on the fast track to juvie hall, Domino had been snapped up by a secret government agency, called, unimaginatively, The Agency, and was offered a chance to not only survive, but to flourish. On her first mission, she'd been dropped into a teeming city on the other side of the world where she didn't know the language, didn't know the topography, didn't know if the people crushing in on her might rob, stab, rape or kill her. She'd been resourceful. She learned quickly. She'd survived. Soon, she'd started to enjoy the challenge of fading into crowds, disappearing into the darkness, manipulating her surroundings until she emerged at the target point victorious.

Over time, she'd gotten sassy. Confident. She'd taken pleasure in screwing with her trainers, breaking into their assignment logs and making alterations that gave her an advantage. She'd learned to cheat out of amusement more than any inability to perform as ordered. She'd immediately been handed over to Darwin for the rest of her training and her life hadn't been the same since.

When she'd turned seventeen, the assignments had changed as well.

The tests became real—matters of life and death.

Mostly death.

And she'd stopped screwing around.

Well, sort of.

Domino stealthily approached the service elevator, noting the guard lurking to the left beneath a burnt-out lightbulb, puffing on an orange-tipped cigarette. Amateur. She should take a few minutes to teach the guy a lesson on effectively remaining out of sight, but instead she opted to scare the shit out of him by approaching in utter silence and then shouting the prearranged password.

"St. Valentine."

The guy jumped ten feet before fumbling his weapon into a halfway-decent defensive stance, his smoldering cigarette butt inches from her foot. Sliding her hands into the pockets of her jacket, she squelched the instinct to disarm him and knock him unconscious and instead, simply snuffed out the flame of his cigarette with her pencil-thin heel. For some reason, Darwin didn't appreciate when she schooled his lower-level agents in the dangers of daydreaming while on duty. The hospital bills probably ate holes in his budget.

The guard stuttered the prearranged response, then slid a key card into the slot beside the elevator. By the way he kept staring at her from over his shoulder, she doubted his sudden inability to keep his eyes off her had anything to do with her sneaky approach.

The elevator swooshed open and she walked inside, her hips swinging just a smidgen more than what was natural. When the doors were inches from closing, she blew him a kiss.

His eyes bulged, and probably other body parts, too.

"Stop teasing my agents, Black." Darwin's voice crackled into the elevator.

"Gotta get my thrills somewhere," she answered.

"From what I witnessed, you got a month's worth of thrills tonight from Luke Brasco."

For effect, Domino wiggled her eyebrows. Darwin didn't respond, nor did she expect him to. So far as teasing went, they'd likely just expended their full store. Though they'd worked together now for nearly fifteen years, Darwin remained coolly aloof. She appreciated the impersonal touch. Despite their long association, Domino knew that at any moment, one of them could disappear and never return. Happened all the time in this business.

The elevator eased to a stop, but she had no idea what floor she was on. The doors remained closed while an infrared beam scanned the interior. Domino remained still, with the exception of an indulgent eye roll. The security measures, while necessary, were tedious. But even after all these years, trust simply didn't exist within The Shadow. There was no tenure, no assumption that years of service equaled loyalty to country or to cause.

Operating under the directive of The Agency, which was run by a group of operatives referred to only as The Committee, The Shadow was a division that didn't exist. Providing top-level tech experts and unmatched assassins and spies, The Shadow executed missions no other investigative service dared touch. Domino had been part of The Shadow since her recruitment, yet she had no illusion that her bosses didn't suspect her of treason on a daily basis, even without proof. Paranoia and constant challenges to loyalty kept them all alive.

The elevator doors sliced open and in a tiny act of defiance, Domino entered the room without her usual recon.

"Quite the risk-taker, aren't you?" Darwin said from behind his desk, a long, sleek table of polished steel.

Domino shrugged. "It's why you love me." She hopped into a curved leather chair and kicked her feet onto the desk, crossing them at the ankles. "Did you catch all the action? I was hot."

"Paris Hilton would be proud."

"Paris Hilton? Isn't she the one who foiled one of our missions when she let her little dog get loose at a soiree in London where a certain terrorist sympathizer was scheduled for termination? The woman needs a leash."

Darwin smirked. "And you're still smarting because I didn't allow you to have a little fun with her as retribution. I hate to remind you, again, that neither one of us is in this business for fun."

"That's the truth," Domino muttered, though Darwin, of course, heard every snarky word.

"Report," he ordered.

"I'm in."

"You know this, how?"

Domino leaned forward. "Hell, Darwin. When's the last time you got laid? Didn't you see the guy? He wanted me so bad, he could taste it."

"All I saw was a business owner who was slightly intrigued by one of the hundreds of beautiful women in his club."

She cursed inaudibly. Darwin didn't approve of certain four-letter words. "Two weeks ago, you ordered me to pique the interest, sexually speaking, of one Luke Brasco. Two weeks and several changes of hair color, clothing style and attitude later and I've finally accomplished the directive. Trust me, if I show up at Club Cicero again like this," she said, sweeping her hands down her scantily clad body, "he'll roll out his tongue like a red carpet."

Darwin pursed his lips just visible within his dark mustache and close-trimmed beard. After a momentary staring contest, Darwin nodded.

"Engage display," he ordered to no one, yet the flat-screen monitor instantly slid up from inside Darwin's desk, forcing Domino to move her legs aside. Finally! Operating without knowing the final objective of her assignment was not the way she usually worked, but this case had been unusual from the first. She'd merely been ordered to attract the attention of club owner, Luke Brasco, with no indication what his part in this play would be. Contact? Dummy? Target? Now, she'd find out.

Domino watched photographs of Brasco flash on

the screen in front of her and enjoyed the view rotating in high-definition color. He was, without doubt, a breathtaking man. Hair the shade of a polished Glock barrel. Blue eyes as sharp as a finely honed blade. Cheekbones that could slice open a vein, and a scar across the bottom of his chin that drew her curiosity. Definitely a man she'd enjoyed watching over the past two weeks.

"Is he my target?"

What a shame it would be to remove such a fine specimen from the gene pool.

"Unknown at this time," Darwin responded.

That caught her attention.

"Explain," she requested.

"The Agency has intel connecting Club Cicero to the sale of classified government secrets."

"Our government?"

"Not exclusively, not at first. Over the past two years, however, the information sold inside the Club has resulted in the death of four Agency operatives and sabotaged three covert antiterrorist operations in three separate countries."

Domino sat up. This was serious shit.

"Why haven't you closed the place down?"

Darwin's frown deepened. "Took us a damned long time to find the common denominator in all the stolen secrets cases. If we move in too fast, whoever is bartering in classified information will simply move to another location and we might not find them again."

"Is it Brasco?"

"Unclear. We have an informant with ties to a spy

network out of Bahrain who identifies the 'bar owner' as the source of the information."

Domino narrowed her gaze. "That's not very specific."

"The informant is low-level and not entirely reliable, which is why we aren't simply sending you in for the kill. Brasco has gone to great lengths over his lifetime to disassociate himself from anything remotely criminal. This is either a genuine effort to stay clean or an elaborate ruse. You need to insert yourself deep into Brasco's life, investigate him and find evidence that he's the source. If he is, eliminate him. If he isn't, find out who is and eliminate them."

She nodded. Simple enough. And yet…

"This isn't my usual type of assignment."

Darwin glanced at the computer screens to his left, then at the pristine blotter on his desk.

Domino sat up straighter. She'd never known Darwin to avoid her gaze, even for a split second.

"You're moving up in the world," he replied cryptically.

Domino bit the inside of her mouth. Bullshit. She'd been nothing but a killer from the start and she saw no reason why The Committee would make any changes. As far as she knew, The Committee was made up of the highest-level operatives from The Agency. She'd once heard that changeover within The Committee happened regularly, to keep any one group from amassing too much power. Conversely she'd also heard the same five anonymous operatives had sat in judgment of their operations since The Agency's inception. She hadn't much cared who was calling the shots so long as her job remained stable and she had someone reliable to watch her ass. Which she had.

"I haven't requested a change in status," she pointed out.

Darwin clucked his tongue. "After all this time, Domino, you know The Shadow doesn't honor requests. Changes in status are up to The Committee."

With nothing further to say on the matter, Darwin tapped the screen in front of him, which changed the images on the display. A shot of the entrance to Club Cicero came into view, complete with the snakelike line of wannabe patrons. Domino pushed aside the questions zinging through her brain to concentrate on his additional briefing.

"Despite the fickleness of the club crowd, Brasco's popularity hasn't waned since he first opened Cicero four years ago."

She chewed her bottom lip. "The place was hopping," she confirmed. "Huge mix of demographic. People in and out. VIPs ushered to backrooms. I can see where it would be hard to keep track of who is buying government secrets there."

"Even harder to figure out who's selling them," Darwin grumbled.

"How long has the bar been under surveillance?"

"Six months."

"Six months?" Domino grunted. She knew she often wasn't pulled into operations like this until The Shadow had exhausted all other options, but six months? How long did it take to figure out if a drop-dead gorgeous bar owner was a legitimate businessman or a traitor whose trafficking in national security secrets was costing the lives of agents all over the world? "Who'd you assign to the job, Inspector Clouseau?"

"Keystone Kops, apparently. That's why we need you."

She arched a brow. "I'm not the right kind of agent for this job."

Darwin nodded decisively, his close-cropped hair remaining perfectly in place. "By the end of this operation, you'll be exactly the agent we need." He slid a thin device across the desk to her. It looked remarkably like an iPod. It wasn't.

"Brasco's dossier has been downloaded into this PDA. Memorize the information, and then wipe it clean."

After checking that her passwords worked, she slipped the gadget into the small nylon duffel at her feet. Preparation was Darwin's forte.

"You'll go in as a photographer on temporary assignment in Chicago. Your equipment will be available once you're in, but your credentials are in the pack beneath your chair."

"Specific considerations?"

"Brasco has two floors of rooms for rent above the club. The entire top floor belongs to him. The second floor has three rooms—one is occupied by his stepmother and one is rented to a pair of nurses out of Rush University Community Hospital. The third was rented by an ambulance-chasing lawyer who suddenly found himself facing a laundry list of fraud charges. He's decided to take off for a little while."

Domino grinned. "So Mr. Brasco suddenly needs another tenant?"

Darwin arched a brow, but his lips remained in a tight line. "Conveniently, yes."

She chuckled, reached down and retrieved the backpack, ignoring the duffel she knew contained her new wardrobe. In the inner pocket, she found a wallet with her new identity. She flipped through the credit cards and fake family pictures, but stopped at the Illinois driver's license.

"Domino Black?" she questioned.

"That is your name."

"Technically, no."

"Exactly. I thought you'd appreciate the humor."

She flipped the wallet closed. "You don't have a sense of humor."

"Apparently, neither do you."

Darwin touched the screen laid flat in front of him, bringing up two gore-infused photographs of headless torsos tinged orange with desert dust.

"Two undercover agents were beheaded in Karachi last night," Darwin explained. "According to this so-called informant, Brasco or someone within his operation is about to sell the names of eleven other Shadow operatives deeply imbedded in Europe and the Middle East. Every foreign operation we have could be at risk."

Domino's blood chilled. "Why don't you pull them out?"

"And risk operations we've worked on for a decade? Can't be done. The agents understand their lives are at risk. But we'd like to save them if we can by protecting their identities."

Domino would say nothing more on that track. Yes, agents for The Shadow accepted that death might be the ultimate payoff for years of risk and intrigue. Still, Shadow agents didn't normally go down without a fight and she was ready, willing and able to take up their cause. She tossed the ID in the backpack and gave the screen a cursory glance.

She must have been frowning, because Darwin stood and walked to the other side of his desk. "We get that you aren't accustomed to this sort of investigation. You're usually in and out within a day. This one could take longer. But I don't have an agent more suited for this operation. I don't want any mistakes and I don't have time to send in two teams. I need one-stop shopping."

Domino nodded, accepting that she'd do whatever necessary to stop the traitor. She'd been trained on the investigative side of covert operations, but she didn't much like going undercover, running interviews and interrogations and answering to contacts on the outside who would then advise how to proceed.

She preferred the simpler assignment. One goal. One job. Go in, take out the target, get out. No reports. No questions asked.

She tapped the screen in front of her and enlarged the still picture of the man she would pursue. Best part of the deal was that he was certifiably yummy. Even if she had to kill him eventually, he was easy on the eyes.

"He's mole material?" she asked.

"To the untrained eye, he's an average Joe."

Domino licked her lips, tapping the screen again until a picture of this Lucas Brasco outside his club washing windows, shirtless, came into view.

"Average isn't the word I'd use. He's more like… tasty."

"I'm glad you think so, because you'll likely have to sleep with him to get close enough to find out if he's our man."

She made sad little clucking noises that weren't sad at all. "It's a dirty job, but someone has to do him."

"That same someone might also have to eliminate him."

Domino glanced up at Darwin. She would have thought that after a decade and a half of working with this man, he wouldn't look at her that way each and every time he gave her an order to kill. The tight lips. Narrowed eyes. Clutched jaw. Tense shoulders. As if she'd refuse the assignment. As if she'd protest against the murderous act she'd built her entire career—hell, her life—around.

She flicked off the screen, kicked her heels off of the desk and stood, loving the feel of her long, lean legs in her new Prada boots. She didn't get much of a chance to wear such sleek designs while on the job so when she was between assignments, she enjoyed the thrill of walking through headquarters in tight leather pants and a tailored jacket, four-inch heels and opaque shades. The weight in the air would shift around her as the density of male pheromones invaded her space. It was a cheap thrill, Domino knew, but a woman with a life like hers had to take what she could get.

"What's my deadline?" She leaned forward on the desk and winked. "And I mean that literally."

Darwin nodded. He understood. Once again, Domino was willing to break the sixth commandment—thou shalt not kill—on behalf of her country.

"We believe that the party most interested in purchasing the names of the operatives is set to contact Brasco sometime in the next two weeks. We're waiting for verification."

"The unreliable informant again?"

Darwin sneered. "We want the person peddling the secrets and that classified information both destroyed before then, or shortly thereafter."

"A sting?"

"Last resort. The club is filled with civilians. That type of operation is hard to contain."

She slung the duffel over her shoulder, picked up the backpack and headed toward the door. "Two whole weeks, huh? So generous," she said, her voice lilting with sarcasm.

Darwin's mouth didn't move. He squeezed his final orders through those tense lips. "Do the job, Domino."

She waved her hand at him dismissively, trying to ignore the instinct that told her this job, unlike all the others, would change her life forever.

"I always do, Darwin. I always do."

LUKE STARED at the ledger until the numbers swam. Handwritten twos, sevens and nines did breaststrokes, backstrokes, swan dives and twirls worthy of an aquatic Olympic event. He slammed the heavy leather cover shut and tossed his pencil so that it skittered off the bar and clattered to the floor.

"You ought to use your computer for that shit," Mikey suggested, emerging from the storeroom where he'd been helping Gloria inventory stock.

"I hate computers," Luke grumbled. The damned things had been the reason for his brother's downfall. Marcus's conviction was the most recent felony in the Brasco family history, which had been marred by arrests, prison terms and odd disappearances for as far back as Luke could remember. If he could stave off the Brasco family curse by denying himself technological advances, then so be it.

Luke slipped off the bar stool, grabbed the errant pencil and shoved it between the pages of the book for his accounts receivable. He'd deal with this later. Tomorrow. Maybe by then, the enchantress's spell would have worn off and he would be able to keep his mind on his work.

"I'd help out, boss," Mikey drawled, "but I'm about as friendly with basic math as a dyslexic chimp."

Luke ran a hand through his hair and chuckled. Normally he had no trouble making the numbers balance out. For the past two years, Club Cicero had operated in the black. Well, more like a dark gray. But since last night, the only numbers Luke had been able to keep in his head were the precise time codes stamped in the lower right corner of a certain security tape.

"Did you look at that tape I left for you?" he asked.

"The one of the chick dancing?" Mikey replied. "She's hot."

His security specialist made the announcement with deep-throated, unabashed lust in his voice. Luke knew the feeling.

"I hope you say that with the same enthusiasm when you're talking to your wife," Luke quipped, emphasizing the last word in his inability to contain the pang of competitiveness that swept through him. Over a woman he didn't know. A woman he didn't dare pursue.

That would be asking for trouble.

Mikey's lips pulled tight against his battle-weary face. "Katie's not exactly open to many compliments about her physical appearance right now."

Luke shifted uncomfortably. He really didn't want to discuss Mikey's personal life with him. Once he went down that road, he'd have to reciprocate. But he'd opened the can of worms regarding Mikey and his new wife. Might as well fish until he caught something. Maybe dealing with someone else's problems would take his mind off his own.

"She's pregnant with twins," Luke pointed out. "I don't suppose it's easy for her to believe that she's anything but—"

"Fat and tired?"

"Ouch. She's having your babies, man. Show a little compassion."

"I do!" Mikey insisted, "I don't think she's fat. I mean, she's fat, don't get me wrong, but it's sort of required. And it's cute, you know? But damn, if I say anything nice to her, she jumps down my throat."

"Which explains," Luke said, glancing at his watch, "why you're here two hours before your shift."

Mikey nodded. "She won't be getting much alone time once the twins are born. I figured I'd give her a little space until then."

Luke didn't even attempt to comment on Mikey's decision. When it came to relationships, he had no clue how they were really supposed to work. None of the men in his family ever did. His own mother had separated from his no-good father when Luke was only two, and when she'd died four years later, Luke had been sent to live with the father he didn't remember and his new wife, Gloria, who had known as much about child rearing as he did at age six. Even after Marcus was born, Gloria had done the minimum of mothering, leaving the tough stuff to their father, who was barely ever around.

Shortly after Luke's tenth birthday, his father had disappeared for good. No letters, no cards…no body. The only thing he'd left behind were the questionable deeds to various plots of real estate around the city and a trust that promised, surprisingly, to take care of his kids. Despite the abandonment and lack of maternal instinct, Gloria had given Luke a home and for that he'd always been grateful. She'd cared for him and Marcus in the best way she knew how, which often meant stashing them in the coat check room of various clubs so she could party, which was where Marcus had honed his pickpocketing skills while Luke watched how the businesses operated.

Just before Luke's twenty-first birthday, Gloria had had Lorenzo Brasco declared legally dead. Nice birthday gift, though her gesture had resulted in a hefty influx of life insurance money, some of which Gloria had lent him to start the first of many businesses in this very building. Situated in Chicago's North End, the prime real estate he'd inherited from his father's trust had been the last legacy of a cursed man.

A legacy Luke wasn't going to blow. A lot of developers wanted the building and he'd lose it if he didn't keep up the mortgage he'd taken in order to outfit Club Cicero in style.

"So what did you think?" Luke asked. "Other than that she's hot. That part I know."

Took Mikey a minute to catch up with the shift in conversation. The guy had a kind heart and a wicked left hook, but his brains were limited to security issues—which was why Luke had let him watch a few moments of the security tape.

"What more can I tell from the tape?" Mikey asked.

"Ever seen her before?"

Mikey squinted as he thought. "Don't think so. She do something?"

Yeah, she'd done something all right. She'd sparked a libido that Luke had thought barely ignitable. He was, after all, surrounded by fabulously beautiful women on a nightly basis—and yet, he normally kept his distance from them, having instituted a hands-off policy since his breakup with Cecily.

Well, not hands-off, exactly. He'd had sex. It was more like a hearts-off policy. A man who lived under a curse like the one handed down from Brasco man to Brasco man shouldn't mess around with things like commitment. He'd tried once and it was, to date, the biggest failure of his life.

But since watching his mystery woman dance last night, every square inch of him was turned *on*.

Frustrated with his inability to squelch the animal cravings coursing through him, Luke grabbed the ledger, opened it to the page marked with the pencil and pretended to peruse the columns once again in search of an elusive numerical discrepancy.

"If she shows up again," he ordered without looking up, "I want you to let her right in. Show her into the VIP room and then let me know she's there."

He ended his request with crisp decisiveness, so he was a bit surprised when Mikey didn't immediately respond with an affirmation. When he looked up and caught Mikey with his eyes and mouth wide-open, he turned behind him and saw why.

She leaned on her left hip and slid her hand exotically down her jean-clad thigh. Today, she was wearing dark, indigo blue. But he'd know her anywhere.

His mystery woman.

He closed the ledger and stood, transfixed. Alert. Aroused.

"Can I help you?" he asked, surprised by the husky voice that emerged from his mouth. He cleared his throat and cursed being born male with no lack of control over the most basic of responses.

She stepped forward and smiled. Well, it was almost a smile. Sly and full of carnal knowledge, the tiny curve of a grin plucked at the wire she'd strung within him last night.

"Actually," she replied, "I'm here to find out how I can help you."

3

MIKEY RETREATED until his lower back hit the edge of the bar. A stool screeched against the floor, but neither Luke nor the sexy chick who'd come into the club seemed to notice. He should leave. Now. Before he screwed this up for Luke somehow—like hitting on her himself.

Not that he would, he thought, as he scrambled through the double doors that led to the kitchen. The weight of the air lightened. Been a long time since he'd had the air sapped out of him just from a woman's presence. Three years, to be exact. Since he'd first met Katie. At the gym, on a Monday morning just after New Year's. She'd been hungover, but determined to find a new personal trainer to help her work off the extra ten pounds she'd supposedly packed on during the holidays. He chuckled to himself, remembering how at the time, he'd wondered how anyone in the world would consider her overweight, least of all her. Sure, she'd had curves, but they were the kind that made men drool.

"Hey, Mikey. What's put such an adorable smile on your face so close to opening?"

His chest tightened as Sienna Monroe sashayed into

the kitchen from the employee lounge in the back, her pin-striped cocktail apron tossed over her shoulder and her black blouse unbuttoned down to the edge of her lacy bra.

"Hey, Sienna."

He stood up straight and gave her a curt nod.

She arched a brow, then frowned prettily. "Aw, now the smile is gone." She closed the distance between them in slow, purposeful steps, until her breasts, generously straining against the remaining buttons, nearly brushed his chest. "What exactly does a girl have to do to bring it back?"

She flicked her finger just under his chin, her flaming red fingernail rasping against his skin like a newly lit match.

Trouble with a capital T. From the first night Luke had hired her, Mikey had tried to stay clear. He wasn't a smart man, but he usually did okay in the common sense department.

He took a step back. "Gloria needs help finishing up the inventory in the storeroom."

Sienna's eyes, emerald-green and lined with black, flashed with disappointment. "Are you trying to get rid of me?"

"Sienna, look." He'd put this off long enough, right? Sienna had been flirting with him nonstop since she joined the Club Cicero staff a year ago. A sassy theater-arts major at DePaul University, Sienna was undeniably desirable. Sexy, too, though not quite like the clearly more experienced woman in the club with Luke, but sensually inviting like any girl who wielded unbound sexual power. And Sienna definitely threw her sex around—even toward him, the wrong guy.

A guy with a pregnant wife.

"You know I'm married, right?"

She didn't back away an inch. "Yeah, you've mentioned it a few times. But I've never once seen your wife come into the club. Isn't she interested in your work?"

"This isn't my only job."

Sienna took a step back and then stretched downward with a resigned sigh, sweeping her hand down to wipe a piece of imaginary dust off her boots. "I've been thinking about finding a new place to work out. The university gym is lame."

The purposeful elongation of her body gave him a perfect view of her tight ass. As a trainer, he couldn't help but appreciate the physical perfection. As a man, he couldn't help the constriction in his groin. As a husband, he cursed his weakness.

He cleared his throat and tried to remember exactly what he had to do before the club opened. He was losing it. And he'd be officially certifiable to even think about screwing around on Katie. She was going to be the mother of his children. He loved her.

"Yeah, university gyms usually are a waste," Mikey said, then changed the subject. It was bad enough he had to deal with her flirting at the club. The last thing he needed was Sienna hanging around his gym. "You gonna help Gloria? I have a few systems to check upstairs."

"I could help you," she purred.

Yeah. Okay. Locked up in the tiny surveillance room with a babe who was clearly hot for him? Not likely.

"No, can do. You know Luke doesn't like anyone up there except me and my staff."

"He lets Gloria watch the cameras."

"She's his stepmother. You gonna argue with him?"

Her shoulders drooped. "Fine. I'll help Gloria. But if you have a free moment during my break, maybe we can talk more about what kind of personal workout I should do. You know, for my body type and all?"

She skimmed her hands down her sides and over her slim waist, winked, then sauntered out of the kitchen. As the doors swung shut behind her, she turned one last time just to see if he was watching her hip-swinging retreat.

And he was. Damn it. She'd caught him.

Again.

LUKE GESTURED TOWARD the bar stool beside him. His mystery woman dropped a duffel and backpack next to her feet, and then slid onto the slick, polished wood chair. Her expression was inscrutable.

"So," he said, trying to play it cool when in fact, heat was spreading through his body with the speed and intensity of a wildfire on parched grass. "How can you help me?"

"I hear you have a room to rent."

"Really?" he asked, surprised. He'd only found out yesterday, via a quickly scribbled note, that his tenant had taken off for parts unknown. Luke hadn't had a chance to advertise his vacancy or even ask if any of his staff needed a new place to stay. "Where'd you hear that?"

She shimmied into a more comfortable position in the chair, then leaned ever-so-slightly closer, just enough for him to catch a whiff of her exotic cologne. Spicy, like cinnamon, but mixed with something bolder, darker…something he couldn't name. "Does it matter? Do you have a room in need of a tenant?"

"As a matter of fact, I do."

"Well, I have *cash*," she said, emphasizing the word. "Looks like we're made for each other."

She'd moved closer—he could feel it. Or had he imagined it? Did he simply want to experience the aura of her body heat so much that he'd created the warmth all on his own?

She glanced up at him through long, dark lashes. Close-up, her eyes were as indigo as her clothes. Dark, mysterious blue with flecks of silvery gray that made her irises glitter.

"So, shouldn't you show me?" she asked.

He swallowed, forcing moisture back into his mouth.

"Show you?"

"The room?"

"Right."

He dashed off the elevated chair and held out his hand to help her with her things. She shrugged into the backpack and cradled the duffel on her elbow then stared at his hand with a quirked brow.

Independent. Right. Got it.

The vacant room was just above the club, so he led

her to the narrow staircase behind the storeroom. Luckily Sienna and Gloria were so engaged in their work, they didn't notice them scoot by.

He breathed a sigh of relief when they reached the second floor. Luke didn't owe his stepmother any explanations and he certainly didn't have to answer to her opinion with regard to who he did or didn't rent rooms to, but his life would be a whole lot easier if she remained in the dark until after the deal was done.

And despite all his instincts telling him this woman was trouble, he couldn't wait for her to move right in. He'd deal with the consequences later.

"So, have you lived in Chicago long?" he asked, digging into his pocket for the master key.

She glanced down the narrow hallway, but he couldn't tell what she thought about the building. It was old and could use a new coat of paint in the hallway, but it was clean. That much he insisted on.

"I'm back after being gone for a while," she replied. "No more ties here."

Luke unlocked the door, standing up straighter as she brushed past. Her cool, almost prickly attitude doused some of the blaze shooting through him, allowing him to think more clearly…and to entertain an inkling of suspicion.

"How did you find out about the room?" he asked again.

"Met Carson Mathers at the airport yesterday," she answered.

Carson had been the previous tenant.

"What an odd coincidence."

She strolled absently around the room, which didn't take long. Consisting of little more than a bathroom with shower, a double bed near the window, a dresser and desk, a television mounted in the corner and a kitchen behind a curtain that had a mini-fridge, a microwave, a hotplate and a sink, the room was sparse. But it was also cheap and in a prime Chicago location.

She turned and tossed her things on the bed.

"Carson told me about your club and the room, which is why I stopped by last night to check out the vibe. I like it," she said, her voice husky. "Besides, I'd rather not have to deal with a hotel. I don't know how long I'm sticking around."

"So you'd rather have a lease?" he asked, perplexed.

She inhaled deeply, which drew his gaze instantly to her breasts, sweet and round in a tight blue T-shirt decorated with random sparkles that winked in the light.

She dug into her jacket pocket and pulled out several hundred-dollar bills, which she fanned out like cards. More than enough to cover a week's rent. She stepped boldly forward, and with her gaze glued to his, stuffed the money in the front pocket of his khakis.

"I'll pay week to week, cash on the barrel." She licked her lips. "If that's okay by you."

The moisture that had deserted his mouth flooded back in full force. He swallowed, dug his hands into his pocket and removed the money, waving it in front of her as if he could give up the cash with no regret. Truth was, he could. Or at least, once he found the cause of his accounts receivable problem, he'd be okay, at least for a month. Until then, he needed the income from the apartments to keep Club Cicero financially strong. Still, he had Carson Mathers's security deposit to carry him over in the rent department. Things weren't that tight.

"Why not go for a place that has room service?" he asked, unable to dismiss the oddity of the situation, despite his personal interest in this mystery woman. For the first time in years, a woman had caught more than just his fleeting interest. She'd downright snared him with just one dance, then disappeared like a wraith. And just when he can't get her out of his mind, she shows up needing a place to live. A temporary place.

She sidled up closer until her fingers danced along the waist of his jeans, just inches from his crotch. "I want to be in the middle of the action, if you know what I mean. I'm here to taste the *real* Chicago again. No hotel fantasies. I'll bet you were born here, too, weren't you?"

Domino slid her hands up his pecs, gave his broad shoulders a devilish squeeze and watched as his pupils had dilated to dusky-blue. She had his interest. Now she just had to close the deal.

"The club downstairs is noisy," he argued.

He was wary. Smart man.

"I remember," she replied.

"You won't get much sleep."

She licked her lips. "I'm a night creature, by nature."

"And what are you by profession?"

Domino lifted a brow and backed away, breaking the spell binding them together, a spell woven from pure sexual attraction. Maybe her target wasn't just some stooge easily diverted with overt sexuality. He was feeling the vibe as strongly as she, but he was strong enough to pull away.

Fascinating.

"I'm a photojournalist."

He eyed her bags. "Those don't look like cameras."

"My equipment's with a friend. I wasn't about to lug it on the L if you'd already rented the room."

He nodded, but didn't speak. He wanted to believe her. The signs were obvious. The way he pocketed the money again. The way he watched her through slightly hooded eyes, his expression almost sheepish for questioning her story. The way his erection pressed against the seam of his pants.

"How long do you think you'll be here?"

Time to up the ante. She hummed, pretending to think as she shrugged out of her jacket and tossed it on the bed. She lifted her arms, stretched, turned toward the window, just to make sure he had a clear view of the tattoo inked onto the lowest low of her back.

"Could be a week, maybe longer. Maybe just a few days. Depends on what the city shows me."

When she turned around, she spied color rising from the V at his neckline.

"What do you think?" she asked, closing the distance between them again. "Will Chicago show a prodigal daughter something interesting this time around?"

He snagged her around the waist and only years of training kept her from yelping in surprise. His hand felt strong against her back. Hard. Insistent. Yet warm. Like he could break her in half if he wanted to—but he most definitely didn't want to.

"I think the city might have something," he whispered, his breath teasing her cheek, "or someone—to interest you. If you know where to look."

A sudden stutter in her chest caught Domino unaware. She remained still, but glanced quickly at his hands to see if he'd administered anything to her skin to cause her heart to race. A split second later, she realized he'd done nothing more than drug her with good, old-fashioned masculine arrogance.

She grinned. "Can I count on you to show me around, then?"

He nodded, released her and strode the three steps he needed to reach the door. "I'm sure I can arrange a private tour. We'll start with the club."

The distance was good. She'd experienced a moment of foggy judgment thanks to this sexy club owner. She needed a chance to regroup. "I'd love it, after I pick up my equipment."

He opened the door and gestured to the hall. "I'll have a key waiting when you get back."

She picked up her backpack and duffel.

"You can leave those here. I'll keep the place locked until you return."

She shook her head, smiling. Fifteen minutes ago, she might have taken him up on his offer. When she'd first spied him last night, she'd figured he probably wasn't the type to be suspicious of a sexy woman who walked in off the street and immediately wanted to live under his roof. No man would question the appearance of his dream woman, right?

Wrong.

There was more to Luke Brasco than met the eye, that was for sure.

She shouldered the duffel. "I need some of this stuff, but thanks." She eased past him, careful to let her back and shoulders brush against his chest. "See you later?"

"Definitely."

She exhaled softly, creating the impression that his nearness sapped her breath. Not that the lie was very far from the truth. She turned the doorknob leading to the stairwell when he stopped her with a quick, "Hey."

She turned slowly. "Yes."

"You didn't tell me your name."

"No, I didn't."

And with that, she hurried down the stairs.

"WHO WAS THAT?" Gloria asked, bursting out of the stairwell after his mystery woman disappeared.

Luke glanced down at the keys he'd been jangling in his hand. Just how long had he been standing here, staring after her?

"New tenant."

Gloria's drawn-in eyebrows shot up high on her forehead. "What happened to Carson?"

"He bailed yesterday."

"Why?"

"No clue. But apparently, he met the woman you just saw at the airport and told her about the apartment. She needed a place, so…"

"So he's not coming back," Gloria said, her voice speculative.

Luke pulled the door shut and made sure the lock

was engaged. "He said in his note that he wasn't. He didn't say anything to you before he left?"

"Carson wasn't very talkative," she replied.

"Even with you?"

She dug her hands onto her hips. "You think I can have a conversation with a brick wall, don't you?"

He grinned. "I happen to know you can. I've seen it."

"I was probably schnockered at the time."

With no need to respond to the obvious, Luke strode to the stairwell.

The mystery woman's scent lingered in the air. He breathed deeply as he jogged down the steps, wondering at her motivation for not sharing her name. He couldn't say he didn't like the mystery. More than likely, she simply had keyed into his fascination with her and enjoyed the tease. But as a landlord, renting with cash to a woman who hadn't yet shared the most basic personal information was probably an incredibly stupid idea. But she'd be back. Or at least, he hoped so.

"So who was the chick I saw leaving?"

"I told you. New tenant."

"Does she have a name?" his stepmother asked.

"Of course."

"And are you going to tell me what it is?"

He spun around as they entered the storeroom. He snagged the completed inventory sheets on the clipboard by the door and scanned the information. Lord, they were going through vodka like prohibition was making a comeback.

"Hey, can you push the rum drinks tonight?"

"This is Chicago, not Miami. And you still didn't tell me her name."

"Why are you so interested?"

"I live here. And I still own part of this building."

A very small part. "You can interrogate her when she gets back with her stuff. I have work to do," he said, beelining toward his office. "Push the rum!"

Gloria grumbled behind him, but he'd made a clean escape. He couldn't share the woman's name if he didn't know it. For that matter, he didn't know if one ounce of what she *had* told him had been the truth, but what could possibly be her ulterior motive for lying about being a free-spirited photographer descending on the city of Chicago for an unspecified amount of time?

Robbery? Fraud? Embezzlement? Had she come in simply to case the joint? Maybe restart that drug operation he'd shut down the year before last?

His mind burgeoned with countless nefarious possibilities, the offshoot, he figured, of being the first in a long line of Brasco men to have a clean criminal record. He hated the cynicism his family had left as his legacy, but sometimes, such distrust came in handy. Made him wary. Cautious. Safe.

Not to mention closed off. Lonely. Asleep to the possibilities around him. A woman like his new tenant might just be the wake-up call he needed.

Cursing as he approached his tiny office tucked behind the dance floor, he skimmed through the locks with quick efficiency. Some of the luster had dulled off his attraction to his mystery woman—and he could only hope the shine would return when she did.

DOMINO TIMED HER reappearance for just after midnight. Via the ancient fire escape, she made her way inside the room she'd rented and stored her stuff in the closet. After setting a combination stunner/alarm device on the tiny storage space, she changed clothes, then exited the way she came in so she could make her entrance back into Luke's life through the club. How she'd explain her ability to move in without Luke surrendering a key was a challenge she'd face later.

First, she had to get the man into bed.

After returning to the safe house to collect the photographic equipment she'd need for her cover, she'd checked in with Darwin. He'd informed her that The Committee expected that the potential buyer of Club Cicero's stolen intelligence might make his move in Chicago sooner than expected. Her two-week deadline to meet her objective might be overly optimistic. She had to step things up. One way to immediately ingratiate herself into Luke's life and gain his immediate trust was to seduce her way into his bed.

Surprisingly she'd never made this particular sacrifice before and Domino couldn't deny that the unexpected call to action thrilled her. Sure, she'd flirted and sexed her way out of tight spots before, but she'd never had to go all the way to complete a mission. Her lovers had always been men of her own choosing—and thankfully, Luke Brasco was just the type of man she'd want. Handsome. Independent. Sexy as sin. He'd even preferred one-night stands and quickie sex that satisfied the body and numbed the empty soul.

Yeah, The Committee had definitely picked the right woman for the job.

However, she couldn't help but suspect that she'd been selected for more than just her sex appeal and killer instincts. In fifteen years of working for The Shadow, she'd learned The Committee didn't screw around. Agents were assigned only the tasks that utilized their strengths. In many ways, Domino was a fish out of water on this case, unaccustomed to long-term entanglements and investigative procedure. They'd chosen her for a reason and only one made sense—a promotion.

Domino had never held any illusions about her job as an assassin. Her ability to take a life without regret proved a valuable asset to an organization charged with the most delicate aspects of national security, but she knew her position was on the bottom rung of The Shadow ladder. She'd never thought about moving up before. Until now. What if her performance on this mission predicated a move into a handler position? No. Anyone who read her file would know that directing action rather than being in the thick of it wasn't her style. She had experience in the darkest aspects of their operations. Her expertise would be most helpful in a position higher up. Even, perhaps, on The Committee itself.

Never once had she allowed herself to entertain such an ambition, but now that the idea had entered her mind, she couldn't dismiss it out of hand. Darwin wasn't getting any younger. Neither was she, though she was still at the top of her game. She could offer The Committee an insider's view, fresh blood and perspective. She could make a real difference.

With a roll of her eyes, she realized that her speculation would likely lead nowhere. Still, though a second round of questioning with Darwin this afternoon had yielded no further insight, she couldn't dismiss something in his eyes—something elusive—that triggered each and every one of the finely honed instincts she'd relied on to keep herself one step ahead of the game since the minute she'd left foster care and hit the streets.

She'd kick ass on this mission.

She'd show The Committee what she was really capable of.

Hell, she'd show herself.

With wicked delight, she strode past the long line of people waiting behind the velvet rope to gain entrance to the club. Music pulsed from the thick brick walls, blasting and then receding every time someone opened the double-wide red leather doors. She endured the jibes and venomous stares of the crowd, feeding off their anger as she cut through the system. If they only knew…

The bouncer crossed his bulky arms across an even thicker chest. "And you are?"

She smiled. "Now, you see, that's the big secret. One your boss has been trying to figure out for over twenty-four hours."

"Which boss?" the bruiser said, casting a glance over at Mikey Maldonado, Luke Brasco's head of security and a former National Guardsman who'd returned from tours in Afghanistan and Iraq less than two years ago.

Mikey straightened when he saw her, his gaze both suspicious and guarded. She curled a straight strand of hair behind her ear and quirked a saucy grin.

He opened the door. "Let her in."

She voluptuously mouthed a thank-you, then crossed inside. Just over the threshold, Mikey grabbed her arm, his grip viselike and hard. She might have drilled him if not for the fact that acting like the hired killer she was didn't jibe with the persona she'd created to achieve her objective.

She glanced up at him coolly. "Something I can help you with?"

"The boss is a good guy," Mikey said. "He doesn't need some chick messing with his head."

She stretched upward. "I'm not just some chick. And it's not his head I intend to mess with. Well, not the one with the brain."

With three fingers, she illustrated her point on his wrist. Nothing fancy, just a basic self-defense move any girl should know. Pain fired his eyes and he instantly released her. He was lucky she didn't snap a bone.

"What the…?"

She smiled and patted him on the shoulder. "Man-handling is not cool, got it? Your boss is a big boy. I'm sure he can take care of himself."

She swung around to find herself chest to chest with the man in question.

Luke Brasco.

He was wearing black. Black shirt. Black jeans. Black boots. He'd practically mimicked her look from the night before and she suddenly understood why the combination had been so effective. Against all the darkness, his light blue eyes sliced through her and simmered the blood coursing through her system.

"So you finally returned," he said.

"Said I would, didn't I?"

"Words are cheap."

"Words won't be so cheap when I use them to tell you who I am," she countered.

He leaned forward, his chin brushing against her cheek. "You don't need to tell me, sweetheart. I already know."

4

SURPRISE FLASHED in her eyes and Luke grinned. She wasn't the only one who could be mysterious. She was, however, the only one who knew her name. He'd asked around, showed a picture printed from the video to all the regulars in the club and while a few remembered seeing her the night before, no one had exchanged so much as a word with her. He'd even tried to contact Carson Mathers, but the old emergency number, work number and cell phone number his former tenant had left on his lease no longer worked—adding to the unknown quality that was this woman.

Adding to the desire.

"You may think you know," she quipped. "But you don't have a clue."

On a brisk shot of air, she immediately chilled, marching past him and through the crowd. If anyone didn't get out of her way fast enough, she moved them with a little shove. One woman who didn't appreciate the push rounded on her to protest, but his new tenant had her would-be opponent backing down with little more than a steely glare.

By the time she reached the stairwell and took the first step, he had to lunge to catch her by the elbow.

"What's your problem?" he asked.

The anger he'd caught a glimpse of moments before slid instantly out of her body. She eased up against him. She wasn't a petite woman in terms of height, so one step up from him and they were eye to eye. Breasts to chest. Groin inches from groin.

"My problem is you're taking all the fun out of my little game," she replied.

He arched a brow. "What game is that? Pull the wool over the landlord's eyes?"

She licked her lips and gyrated her hips so that her jean-encased sex brushed hotly against his. "You like blindfolds?"

He chuckled. "I'm not averse to them."

"Even with women you don't know? You *are* the adventurer, aren't you?"

"With the right woman."

"Care to put your money where your mouth is?" she challenged.

"You're assuming you're the right woman."

Laughter erupted from deep in her gut. "I never make assumptions. I'm simply stating a fact."

She turned to dash up the stairs, but he hadn't released her elbow, so he easily waylaid her escape and tugged her against him. She didn't protest, but instead, speared her hands through his hair, grabbed his cheeks with her palms and pulled his lips against hers.

Instantly her tongue slipped into his mouth. The flavor of clean, crisp mint invaded his senses, but the effect was anything but cool and refreshing. The kiss was brief, but so hot, he imagined smoke puffing out of his mouth when she pushed him away.

He cleared his throat. "What was that?" he asked.

"Don't you know?" She moistened her top lip with her tongue, then performed a little flick that invoked a million and a half wicked possibilities. Oh, to feel that tongue on him again. Wet. Skilled. Uninhibited.

"I know that any woman who kisses her landlord without sharing her name first is up to something."

"Are you always so suspicious?"

He crossed his arms tightly over his chest. "Yes."

She made a soft, clucking noise that he only heard because she leaned forward to make sure he didn't miss one sound. "Such a shame to be so young and so jaded."

"I'm not so young."

She grinned. "Neither am I."

With a spin, she took the stairs two at a time, a mighty feat in those killer heels. She stopped at the top and with an impatient look over her shoulder, indicated she expected him to follow.

He shoved his hands in his pockets and feeling his keys beneath his fingers, figured he might as well let her into the room she'd rented. But she didn't stop at the second floor where her room was. She continued to the third floor landing.

His floor. His private domain.

She paused at the door, not even attempting to twist the knob. Did she know he kept it locked 24/7? When you lived over a nightclub, you had to employ extreme measures to ensure privacy.

"This is where you live," she said.

"How did you know?"

"People talk," she said, though all the innocence in her voice was completely incongruous to the picture she presented in the hip-hugging leather pants, lacy blue camisole and short, fitted jacket. A sapphire sparkled from the hoop in her belly button. She leaned saucily against the door, as if having sex right then and there wasn't outside the realm of distinct possibility.

"No one talks to you," he replied, confident in his pronouncement since he'd interviewed just about every regular in the club when fishing for her name.

"You don't know that for certain," she coaxed.

"I do."

She shrugged off his assertion. "Well, perhaps no one spoke specifically to me, but they talk a lot of shit to each other. And I'm an excellent listener."

How come he didn't doubt that?

"Why are you here?" he asked.

"In Chicago or in this stairwell, waiting for you to show me where you live?"

He arched a brow. "Both, though why you bypassed your floor suddenly interests me a lot more."

She leaned in close so that her sweet minty breath skittered across his lips. "Do I have to spell it out?"

He shook his head. "Then let's go back to the first question."

"Why is my personal business so interesting to you?"

"Because my tenant's personal business usually determines whether or not they can pay the rent."

When her tiny frown puckered her lips, Luke's chest tightened. Oh, she was good. Damned good.

"I can pay my rent and then some, trust me. A hip new travel magazine is willing to pay me very well for a series on the city of Chicago."

"You don't sound like that excites you," he commented.

"Since meeting you, other things excite me more."

"Oh, really?"

"You sound so doubtful. Don't you know how attractive you are?"

He smirked. "I've been told."

"Maybe it's time someone does more than tell you. Maybe it's time you turn yourself over to the unknown, surrender to what you know you want, but up until now, have denied."

She undulated her upper body until the short jacket she wore over the lace camisole spilled off her shoulders. She leaned down and in a move that stole his breath, slowly, inch by erotic inch, released an invisible zipper that started at the ankle of her leather jeans and stretched up to her thigh. The move revealed a smooth, bare leg. At the hip, he spied the tiny string of her panties, such as they were.

With a crooked finger, she beckoned him closer. A surge of something instantaneous and chemical, like an explosion in a mad scientist's secret lab, drew him forward. He clutched his keys so tightly in his hand, he'd probably broken skin.

She smiled as he neared and as soon as he was close enough, hooked her arms around his neck and the nearly naked leg around his waist.

Was he crazy? Had he completely relinquished what was left of his common sense in pursuit of a woman with no inhibitions and an obvious agenda, even if he didn't know what it was?

"I don't know your name," he said, as if that fact made any difference whatsoever. Didn't to him. Likely didn't to her, either.

"Ask me," she whispered, running her tongue around the shell of his ear until his skin vibrated beneath her touch.

"What's your name?"

"Domino," she replied.

"Like the game?"

She rewarded him with a slow, moist kiss just at the base of his neck. "Precisely like the game."

"What's your last name?"

"Black," she replied, moving her mouth along his chin erotically. "And before you ask, yes, like the color. Reach into my back pocket."

He groaned, releasing the growing tension just enough to speak. "You have room to put something in the pocket?"

God help him, but her laugh was throaty and deep and irresistible. The sound drilled straight through muscle and bone and injected into his bloodstream until he could practically hear a rush of hot fluid flooding through his ears.

"You'd be surprised at what I can do with tight spaces," she replied.

He reached around her and with a tentative touch, traced the seam until he found the pocket. Unable to resist, he opened his palm and filled his hands with her buttocks. She was firm and curvy, muscled. He guessed she was a runner. Power walks did not these glutes make.

"Find it?"

He blinked. Find?

In her pocket. Right.

When he concentrated, he felt the rectangular outline. With more pleasure than he should have experienced, he slipped two fingers inside her pocket and removed the business card.

Thick stock. Professional lettering. Domino Black, freelance photographer. A phone number. Cell. A Web site address.

"Flip it over."

Three references, one right here in Chicago.

"This could all be fake," he said.

"Of course it could. But it's not. Check on the Web, make a few phone calls and you'll see that I am who I say I am."

"It's after midnight."

"Not in Paris," she said, tapping the second number on the card with her blood-red fingernail.

Her eyes flashed with a challenge no man could possibly resist. He reached around her and inserted the keys into the lock. Once inside, he pressed his security code into the keypad, then flipped on a light and gestured her inside.

She walked slowly, her gait tentative. The air seemed supercharged with electricity. He tried to remember the last time he'd let a woman into his private domain and he couldn't. Since his former fiancée, no woman other than his employees or his stepmother had ever been here. At least, not more than once.

"I'll use the phone in my bedroom. Make yourself at home," he said.

"You might regret saying that," she teased, tossing her jacket carelessly onto his camel leather couch. Then she stretched her arms upward, turning so he spied again what he was certain was a tattoo across her lower back.

His feet rooted to the floor.

She flashed a seductive smile. "Don't tell me. You're a real neat freak?"

No, a tattoo freak.

Without another word, he slipped into his room.

Though he kept the air conditioner at a steady seventy-four degrees, the temperature in his bedroom bordered on hellish. He tamped down the instinct to discard his suddenly sticky shirt and instead, headed for the desk he had tucked in the corner. He dialed the number on the business card and asked, in suddenly clumsy English, for Pierre Louis.

"Mr. Louis?" he said once a male voice, thick with a French accent, said hello.

"It's pronounced Loo-EE, *n'est-ce pas?* Who is this?"

"My name is Lucas Brasco. I'm in Chicago, Illinois. Domino Black has listed you as a reference."

The rest of the conversation was quick, enthusiastic, but not particularly enlightening since Luke lost every three words as Monsieur Louis, a fashion designer apparently, gushed and raved in a wild mix of

French and English about the photographs Domino Black had taken for his spring catalog and Web site. The ebullient man made sure to get in a few words about how trustworthy and hardworking Domino was, which as a landlord, Luke figured he should have been happy to hear. Once he hung up, he couldn't help but entertain a wave of disappointment.

His fantasy woman was real. Flesh and blood.

He threw the phone onto the bed, then stalked back into the living room, stopping dead when he saw her leaning over the back of his couch, checking out the view through the windows.

"Not much to see from here, huh?" she commented.

Luke couldn't reply, though a few words skittered through his brain—some asinine come-on about the view being better inside. He said nothing, his tongue thick and mouth dry as the tattoo he'd spotted on the small of her back came fully into view.

A panther. Sleek and black. Eyes glittering in jade-green. It stalked just below her waist, its sharp claws stretching into those peekaboo leather pants she'd unzipped up the leg.

She glanced over her shoulder and clearly, recognized what had mesmerized him into silence.

"You like? Got it in Bangkok."

He managed a nod. This couldn't be happening. Couldn't be real.

"Did Cecily send you?"

She climbed backward off the couch, giving him a torturous view of her curvaceous, generous bottom as she moved. "Who's Cecily?"

"My ex."

"Ex…wife?"

"Fiancée," he replied.

No way was this a coincidence. Domino had a panther. The very animal he'd encouraged Cecily to choose when she'd decided she wanted a new brand on her skin. She'd chosen a dragon, rejecting his personal request that she pick the sleek jungle cat he'd been fascinated with since childhood. And now here was Domino Black, a total stranger sporting the animal he thought was the ultimate symbol of sexiness. No way.

Tension rammed into his spine and then burst out into his bloodstream like cold steel rods. Would his former fiancée have gone this far? Was she somehow setting him up? He hadn't seen her in months. Their breakup had been her idea, not his, though he couldn't help thinking he'd dodged a bitter bullet.

"Did Cecily send you here?" he asked.

Her face skewed in confusion. "No," she replied, speaking slowly. "I told you. Carson Mathers—"

He held up his hand. Sometimes, his suspicious nature got the best of him.

"Never mind. Just being paranoid."

She nodded, studying him for a moment. "I'm fascinated by the fact that you were once engaged. What happened?"

"The usual. Let me show you to your room."

"I'd rather stay here and explore your room."

"There's nothing to see here."

"Then I'll close my eyes."

She stood mere inches from him and let her lashes

drift softly shut. She took a deep breath, and her breasts rose high, as if in offering. With her head titled gently to the right, Luke's gaze drifted to the supple curve of her neck and all suspicion evaporated like steam.

"What are you doing?" he asked, his voice choked by his fascination.

Damn.

"Shh," she admonished. "You can learn a lot about a man from the sounds in his apartment. The smells. The textures."

Domino concentrated, aware of her power as a seductress…aware of his power to be seduced. She hadn't been lying about utilizing all her senses to explore this man, his space, his wants and needs. Visual observation had always been a key weapon in her arsenal, but Domino had completed many jobs when her eyesight had been either completely useless or hindered by the limitations of night vision goggles or infrared technology. The Shadow offered her the best equipment, but that didn't mean she didn't have to keep her natural instincts honed to razor-sharp capacity.

Especially when in the company of one Luke Brasco.

"You like hot dogs," she said.

The odor was distinct and she imagined there was a greasy pot of water sitting somewhere on his stove. Just like a bachelor.

She didn't have to peek an eye open to hear him sniffing the air.

"Chili dogs, to be precise," she continued.

"Mustard or ketchup?" he asked sardonically.

She laughed and surprisingly, the humor was real. "That's a question? Mustard, of course. No self-respecting Chicagoan would put ketchup on a hot dog."

"No self-respecting American, in my opinion."

"I love ketchup on my hot dogs," she lied. Domino was pretty sure she hadn't eaten a hot dog since childhood.

"You seem like the type to break with tradition."

Tradition wasn't even in her vocabulary.

"Oh, I like some things the old-fashioned way."

"Like?"

He stepped nearer, so she took the opportunity to turn and give him another glimpse of the tattoo that had shocked him earlier.

He growled, this time loudly.

"Like…" She smiled. "Okay, you've got me. I don't like anything the old-fashioned way."

His touch, light and tentative on her lower back just above the tattoo, didn't surprise her, but she allowed a tiny thrill to course through her veins. With only the pad of his finger, he injected fire into her, a fire that hadn't burned in too long.

"How did you know?" he whispered.

She didn't reply, knowing the question was entirely rhetorical. The panther fascinated him. Lured him. Spoke to his deepest fantasies. Fantasies he'd likely never told anyone—except his former fiancée.

As he'd guessed, Cecily Devine had indeed revealed his black panther fantasy. Clearly the man had no idea that his former wife-to-be had kept an Internet blog for the past three years. Took a little hacking to reach into the archives, but The Shadow tech guys were nothing if not thorough.

In her pseudo-private musings, the woman had confessed every last sordid detail about why she'd let this man go. After reading the online journal, Domino could only conclude that Cecily Devine was the worst kind of fool.

Luke Brasco was strong, opinionated and smart—but he didn't need arm candy to bolster his ego or a doormat of a woman to make him feel like a man. He'd reportedly given Cecily the best sex she'd ever had—details Domino had read with interest since, really, every little fact could help her achieve her objective, right? Her plan was simple—seduce Luke as a way of instantly becoming tight with him. Only then could she discover if he was selling the secrets that had cost her fellow agents their lives.

And hell, it had been too long since Domino had taken a lover. Over a year. She'd messed around with Roman Brach, an Agency operative with a lower security clearance than her, but the interactions with him had been all about instant gratification. According to Cecily, Luke had taken things slow…deliciously slow…and despite her hardened heart, Domino couldn't deny herself the titillation of reading every erotic detail.

Erotic details she'd experience for herself if she played her cards right.

"You like my tatt?"

"You have no idea," he said, his hot breath caressing the back of her neck.

"Want to see more?"

She didn't wait for his reply, but unbuttoned and unzipped her pants, then slid them slowly down her body. He remained behind her, his hands braced on her waist, his sex bulging against his slacks so she could feel him hot and hard against her. She stepped out of the pants and kicked them away.

She glanced coyly over her shoulder.

"Go on," she urged. "Take a closer look."

He stepped back and in a move that surprised even her, dropped to his knees. His hands smoothed the cheeks of her bottom, bared by her thong underwear. The lines must have invaded the tattoo, because with gentle, tentative fingers, he lowered the elastic so he could see every line and curve of the artist's rendering.

She hoped the tattoo, a high-quality temporary that couldn't be removed without special chemicals, would look permanent under such close scrutiny. His approving hum as his thumbs traced every curving line, verified she'd passed his test.

"This is amazing," he said.

She lifted the hem of her blouse and yanked it over her head. "Just the tatt or the body beneath it?"

"Both," he replied, then placed a kiss at the center of her back. A hot drop of moisture spilled from between her thighs, catching her unaware. She'd fully expected to enjoy this seduction, but not so quickly or with such heated intensity.

She wiggled her backside in response, spreading her legs just the tiniest bit as she reached around and grabbed his adoring hands. She guided his touch around her bottom, then across to the front, urging one hand to touch her sex through the flimsy material of her panties.

"This is crazy," he said, his mouth pressed against her ass.

"Yes," she agreed. "Crazy is good."

She took his other hand and steered it toward her bare breast. Once the tips of his fingers touched the lower swell, he took over. He adjusted his position, redirecting one hand between her legs so he could torture her completely with one finger pressing nearer and nearer to her clit while the other tweaked and teased a hardened nipple.

He stood and pressed his erection against her. "Tell me what you like."

She inhaled sharply, the request unexpected. With a spin, she twirled on him.

"I like my men naked," she said boldly.

He complied as quickly as possible, tossing his shirt, slacks, boxers, socks and shoes into a haphazard pile on the floor. "How's that?"

She slid her hands down his chest, waist and thighs, feeling the heat emanating off his sex, but denying herself even the quickest touch. For now.

"Perfection. But I sort of liked that game we were playing before. You know, close your eyes and tell me what you see."

He quirked an eyebrow, disappeared into what she assumed was his bedroom long enough to give her time to retrieve a condom from her pocket. With nowhere else to put it, she placed it inside the triangle of her thong, figuring that once that was gone, the prophylactic would be needed.

She could make this fast, she knew. She should get

the sex over with and then continue with the rest of her plan. But why? No one at The Shadow said she couldn't enjoy her interactions with Luke Brasco and so far, she was experiencing the kind of sensual delight few men offered. Her lifestyle demanded sex be fast and direct—just enough to meet the needs for a brief interlude before the participants disappeared into the night. She'd never been ordered to kill a lover before, but in fifteen years, she'd learned to let nothing affect her, nothing surprise her, nothing catch her off guard.

Luke returned with a necktie over his shoulder and a condom in his hand. She couldn't help but grin and slyly remove the foil square she'd tucked into her underwear.

He returned her sinful smile. "Can never be too prepared."

"I like the way you think."

He flicked the tie off his body. "So who wears the blindfold?"

Too easy, she thought, if she insisted he don the mask. "Oh, me. Think you can surprise me?"

The gleam in his eyes told her he intended to try.

Crossing behind her, he carefully placed the tie across her eyes and knotted the material behind her head. "Are you sure you should trust me like this? We hardly know each other."

She licked her lips as he spun her, knowing he was watching. "That's part of the thrill. Just what is this handsome, sexy man going to do to me?"

"What do you want me to do to you?"

The darkness didn't frighten her. Domino had been

tested by men with more dangerous intentions than a hot romp with a willing woman. She couldn't remember ever playing sex games like this before—her sexual adventures had never been so simple, so innately innocent—and yet the newness injected her with daring, coaxing her to relinquish her usual control and distrust. For the first time in a long while, she wasn't calling the shots in the bedroom. At any moment, Luke Brasco could turn the tables, though she had every confidence she could instantly turn them back. But for now, why?

"Get to know me," she replied.

He started with a kiss. Long, hard and hot, he molded his naked body completely to hers, but the only moving parts at the moment were his lips and tongue and teeth. Eventually his hands glided skillfully down her body, cupping her breasts, buoying the weight against the roughness of his skin, flicking her nipples with his thumbs. The action was deliciously uncomplicated and incredibly arousing. He took his time, not averting his sensual assault until she emitted a soft and rebellious coo.

He took her hands. "Follow me."

He guided her across the room, then eased her onto a bar stool. He abandoned her for a second and she heard the flick of a light switch and after a few seconds, felt the warmth from a lamp directly above her. She remembered the layout of the room with complete precision. He'd turned on the canister-shaped fixtures dangling above the bar so that a beam of light illuminated her nearly nude body.

"There we go," he said, his voice rife with pleasure. "You're amazingly beautiful."

She smiled, opening her legs ever-so-slightly, then leaned back tentatively. Finding the bar behind her, she balanced on her elbows so that her breasts jutted forward. "Glad you approve."

He'd stepped away. The air stilled. Except for the music pulsing from far below, silence reigned. She couldn't even hear him breathing. What would he do next, this sexy, unassuming bar owner who might just be in league with international terrorists hell-bent on destroying the world?

When his lips crashed against her neck, she nearly leaped out of her skin. His teeth rasped against her flesh, reminding her that the sensation could have easily been a knife blade wielded to slit her throat. Instinctually she reached for the blindfold. Had she made a dire mistake?

He cupped her breasts again. "Whoa, babe. What tensed you up so fast?"

She swallowed thickly. "You surprised me."

"Isn't that what you wanted?"

Suddenly, slow and torturous didn't work for her anymore. Her heartbeat accelerated and her breath shortened, but not for the reasons he likely imagined.

"Yes," she said.

"Well, you ain't seen nothing yet."

His voice lacked menace of any type and once he wrapped those glorious lips of his around her hardened nipple, she realized he meant her no harm. There was no way in hell he knew who she was, no way he intended to do more than show her the sensual weapons he had at his capable command. He closed in on her, his body wedged between her legs as he flicked and sucked and laved her breasts until all thoughts of danger receded into the background.

He breathed against her belly. "There you go," he said. "You're more relaxed now."

"You're good at this."

He slipped his finger beneath her panties, tickling her intimately, using the moisture pooling from her flesh to intensify every tiny thrust.

"I'd like to think so. You're so wet. And hot. Lift your bottom, sweetheart."

Using her elbows for balance, she complied. He slipped off her panties and then she heard him inhale.

"So musky and sweet."

She opened her legs wider.

He eased his fingers over the smooth skin of her thighs, then tangled into the scant pubic hair she'd left after her waxing. "Will you come if I taste you?"

God, yes. That easily.

"You're tensed up again."

She took a deep breath and corralled her anticipation. "I'm just anxious to feel what you'll do next."

"The choices are endless."

He kissed her neck, suckling at the spot where her pulse leaped until the pressure pounded further downward, in perfect synchronicity.

"Your lips are a little high."

He chuckled. "I like to start at the top and work my way down."

She surrendered to the sensations he invoked, marveling how a single finger drawing circles on her inner thigh—predictable, unwavering, insistent spheres—could entice her so deeply. Just when would his finger stray inside her again? Just how deep would he go? Just how hot would she be once he finally gave her what she so desperately needed?

It wasn't his hand that answered the questions, but his tongue. He instantly sought and found her clit, tight, hot, insistent. With a jolt of electricity, he brought her to the brink and then, when she'd tightened her hands into fists and wrapped her legs over his shoulders, he pushed her over the edge. Colors bright and bursting danced behind her eyelids. Her body shivered, quaked and creamed. She widened her thighs, allowing him complete and total access. The heat from the lamps beamed hot on her wet and swollen nipples, budding them even further. And just when she thought the pleasure would ebb, he grabbed her tits and tightened his fingers over the reddened flesh until she screamed out in pleasure.

She whipped off the blindfold and with a skilled scissor-kick, leaped off the bar stool.

He stood, a cat-in-the-cream smile dancing over his lips.

"You a gymnast in another life?"

Her body vibrated from the intensity of the orgasm, but she knew she could have more. She would have more. Panting, she used the tie to rope him around the neck and pressed her moist, hot body against his.

"I've been a million things in a million lives," she

replied, knowing she sounded like a flaky new age kook—and not giving a damn. She wanted Luke Brasco inside her. It was time to take control.

She tightened the noose and after grabbing the condom he'd left on the bar, ushered him to the bedroom.

He didn't offer any resistance. The man was willing, laughing with her as they entered his private domain. She flung him toward the bed as she released the tie and he fell with a carefree peal of laughter.

She flicked the condom at him.

"Put it on."

He arched a brow over his dilated blue eyes. "Demanding, aren't you?"

"Can't take it?" she challenged.

He peeled the condom package and eased the circular latex over his jutting cock. "I can take anything you can dish out."

She climbed onto the bed, swinging her leg over his waist and easing his sex into hers. "Let's see about that."

Despite the residual quivering in her muscles, Domino used her thighs to lift and drop in a slow, languorous rhythm, enjoying every inch of him inside her, every sensation of the friction between their bodies. She reached behind and teased his balls, grinning as his moans intensified.

He grabbed at her hips, but she slapped him away, then leaned forward on his chest. "Hang on there, cowboy. I'm setting the pace here."

His expression was a mix between a grin and a

scowl, as if he didn't know whether to protest or rejoice. "I've got to do something with my hands."

"Use your imagination."

He slid his palm down his own chest and found her hot center. Fire exploding behind her eyes, she nearly bucked right off of him, but she managed to maintain control. When he squeezed her left nipple, hard, with his other hand, her entire nervous system shifted into overload. She might have closed her eyes. She might have forgotten to breathe. The only thing she knew for sure was that she maintained the slow pace of her ride—for about five more seconds.

After that, she lost all measure of time and space. Their bodies melded and his orgasm became hers and vice versa. His hands seemed to be everywhere at once, touching her, urging her, adoring her. When she finally lost power over her body, she collapsed forward, landing with her lips against his.

And as she did, she twirled the onyx ring she wore on her pinkie, unhinged the stone with an easy flick and jabbed the hidden spike into the side of his neck, directly into his bloodstream.

5

His entire body jerked hard, stiffened and then completely and totally relaxed.

Allowing herself a moment of regret for the additional hours of lovemaking she'd sacrificed for the cause, Domino returned the ring to its usual, normal appearance. She couldn't resist rotating her hips one more time, enjoying the last remnants of his hard body buried deep inside her. Then, she eased slowly down his body, kissing his neck, his pecs, his stomach. When she flicked her tongue over his balls and he didn't move a single muscle, she knew the drug had done its job.

Time to get to work.

But for the first time since she could remember, she didn't bound off the bed and move on to her next task quickly and efficiently. She lingered, enjoying his warmth, unconscious or not, beneath hers. His impressive dick, still elongated and engorged, tweaked her own sex with renewed interest.

She'd had two orgasms tonight already. She'd save the rest for another time, another place. She felt certain she'd screw him again—that is, if she didn't find information in the next two hours that necessitated his elimination.

Taking a few seconds to remove and discard his condom and retrieve the sheets from the floor to cover him, Domino began her search of his apartment. She started with the bedroom, checking every nook and cranny, every drawer top to bottom and even underneath. She turned on as many lights as she could find and inspected the carpeting, looking for any indication that hidden compartments existed beneath the short, dark pile. The bed, especially with Luke's body nestled in it, was too heavy for her to move, but even without his two-hundred-pound frame, she figured even he couldn't budge the thick, teak monstrosity without help. She found a flashlight in the kitchen and checked beneath the bed anyway, satisfied that the layer of dust indicated that no one had disturbed the carpet underneath for a very long time.

She checked the living room next, paying extra attention to the walls. In the bathroom, she found an impressive collection of *Playboy* and *Penthouse*, none recent editions, but nothing that tied him to being the source of secret information. After doing a similarly efficient search of both the living room and the kitchen, she concluded two things of consequence.

First, Luke Brasco was a bachelor of the first order. He fit each and every stereotype ever determined regarding the unmarried male. His refrigerator had nothing but beer, bread and peanut butter. His DVD collection included every action flick ever produced. His little black book needed to be transferred into a PDA or he needed to buy more pages to stuff between the worn leather covers.

And that discovery had led her to her second, more important observation.

Luke Brasco didn't indulge in the latest techno toys.

He had a cell phone—the basic type that had no room to store more than a few numbers. Not surprisingly, a check of his call history revealed that he talked exclusively to his employees. He had a VCR/DVD with the clock still blinking 12:00. He had a clock radio and a stereo equipped with a cassette tape deck and a CD player added after the fact. He had a television with satellite, but no digital recording device.

And most importantly, no computer. No PC. No laptop. Nothing that a successful business owner in the twenty-first century would need to operate on par with the rest of the technology-loving world.

In other words, either Luke Brasco was horribly behind the times, had a techno-phobia like she'd never seen or he wanted everyone to believe that he didn't know a hard drive from a hard-on.

She slipped back into his room and dressed quickly. From the pocket of her jacket, she retrieved her wax box and made impressions of every key on his ring. From the secret compartments in the thick heels of her boots, she removed several wireless surveillance devices, which she placed in random corners of the rooms, watching the angles so that nearly every inch of the apartment was covered, including the bathroom. After climbing onto the top of the toilet to insert the last microcamera into the ventilation grate, she hopped down.

When her heels hit the tile floor, she heard a telltale sound. A hollow rattle.

"In the bathroom?" she asked herself aloud.

Granted, she should have examined the tiles more carefully to begin with, but a quick glance at her watch told her that she had maybe ten minutes to a half an hour before Luke woke up. She barely had enough time to give the apartment one last clean sweep. Instead she dashed to the door and opened it a crack.

He'd rolled over. The sheets were no longer neatly over him, giving her a wide-angle view of his impressive ass. Beneath her blouse, her nipples peaked. Maybe once she checked the floor, she'd strip down, climb into bed and wait until he woke up for another go-around. She had a scheduled check-in with Darwin soon, but what would it hurt if she was a few minutes late?

Unable to contain a rebellious grin, Domino shut the door, turned on the shower to provide cover noise and crawled back to the floor to find the hollow tile.

On a hunch, she opened the nearest drawer and extracted a thin metal nail file. She found a nick in the grout exactly the same dimension as the tip of the file—he'd used this method on a regular basis. With a quick flip, the tile popped off and inside the floor, she found a small safe.

She rolled her eyes. Good, God, she didn't have time for this. She heard a sound that easily could have been movement in the other room. Cursing, she replaced the tile, threw the nail file into the drawer and stripped off her clothes. She'd just doused her hair with water when the door to the bathroom opened.

"Domino?"

Seductively she opened the shower curtain, giving him a full and unhampered view of her wet, naked body.

But judging by the look of him, he was in no condition for sex. He was clutching his head with both hands and buoying his weight by leaning against the doorjamb. Yeah, he'd have a hell of a headache right about now. Common side effect of the knockout drug she'd used.

"Man, you wear out easily," she quipped.

Please, God, don't let me throw up in front of the best lay I've had in months. Make that years. Luke pressed his lips tightly together and willed the bile to retreat from his throat and back into his stomach. What was wrong with him? He didn't remember much after that last orgasm. She'd been on top of him, his hands on her breasts, riding him with unabashed pleasure and then next thing he knew, he'd rolled out of the bed and onto the floor with a cold, dizzying thud.

"I'm sorry. I need to use the bathroom," he explained.

Despite the queasiness roiling through his body, Luke appreciated the sight of Domino slicking her hair back beneath the showerhead before closing the curtain. "I can't hear a thing with this water running."

He didn't have time to decide whether or not to believe her, but instead took care of business as quickly as possible. Sharing a bathroom like this seemed so incredibly intimate, even more intimate than having sex with her. Weird, but true. After he flushed, a soft moan from the other side of the curtain caught his attention, despite the head-splitting pain shooting from temple to temple.

A second moan, this one louder and deeper, drew him to the shower stall. He listened as she emitted moan after moan, interspersed with a sensual coo or a breathless sigh that had an amazing effect on his headache.

Headache? What headache?

He brushed his teeth, swished some mouthwash and popped a couple of aspirin with a palmful of water. The combination of mint overload and curiosity over exactly what Domino was doing in his shower without him renewed his energy and pushed his physical discomfort to the background. He'd sleep it off. Later. Much, much later.

He tore open the curtain to find her standing against the wall with his retractable showerhead in her hand, a hard stream of water aimed between her legs. Her breasts bounced as she panted hard and fast. The woman was insatiable. And damn it, tonight, so was he.

Without hesitation, he stepped into the shower, immediately doused in scalding hot steam. He could only imagine the temperature she was using against her sensitive flesh.

Her eyes fluttered open.

"You don't have to do that all by yourself," he said.

She opened her mouth to speak, but the impending orgasm stole her ability to form any words. Instead she glanced down at the showerhead and made a tiny move that meant, at least to him, that he should take over.

Reaching forward, she grabbed his dick and tugged

him closer, shouting out as the stream of water hit her with more force. She stroked him hard and long and fast. The atmosphere thickened with wet steam and hot need. He kissed her with the same urgency, both of them breaking often to catch what they could of the humid air. Luke didn't think he could come again without being inside her, but he was wrong.

When the explosions ebbed, he dropped the showerhead, which dangled from the faucet and continued to billow steam around them. With his back against the tile and his hand pressed to his chest to still his accelerated heartbeat, he was unprepared when she turned the water on him. She'd adjusted the dial so that the stream wasn't concentrated, but soft and soothing. The temperature lessened as well to a comfortable luke-warm.

He fluttered his eyes open. With her tongue captured between her teeth, she focused the stream lazily across his shoulders so that the water sluiced down his body, wetting every inch of him.

Her gaze lighted on his groin.

"Don't even think about it," he warned.

She grinned, then lowered the showerhead so that she rinsed his thighs, knees and feet. Once he was completely doused, she reattached the showerhead to the wall, grabbed the soap and lathered her hands.

"I can think all I want," she replied. "But I know every man has his limits."

He stole the soap from her slippery hands. "And every woman doesn't?"

She licked her lips and smeared the foamy lather

across his chest. "I like to push beyond my limitations. But, I don't want to exhaust every possibility in one night, either. I mean, what's left for tomorrow if we have each other every which way tonight?"

On that note, they spent the next twenty minutes doing nothing more than bathing, rinsing, drying, kissing and dressing. She allowed him to towel and comb her hair. He allowed her to carefully zip up his jeans and slip on his loafers. By the time they reached her door, they'd created a quiet, comfortable intimacy Luke felt sure he hadn't achieved with Cecily until after they'd been dating a year—if then.

But he wasn't stupid. So much had happened tonight, he needed time to process the details and analyze the consequences. He was no sucker for love, but damn, this woman had made an impression like he'd never experienced. She was, for all intents and purposes, the perfect woman.

And that scared the shit out of him.

Domino watched him reach into his pocket and retrieve his keys. He had no way of knowing she'd already been inside her apartment or that by midmorning, she'd have replicas of all his keys in her possession. She concentrated on the dreamy look on his face, on the satisfied swagger in his walk. She'd not only achieved her goals for the night, she'd excelled. And in return, she'd experienced three orgasms and a comfortable repartee with a man who might be a spy and a traitor to his country, but was still the most skilled and entertaining lover she'd had in years.

He swung the door open for her, inviting her inside

without the presumption that he would follow. She covered her mouth and yawned. The gesture was genuine, but also acted as a reminder that it was nearing dawn and they'd both be better served by going to bed. Alone.

"Thanks for the warm welcome," she said, turning and commandeering the doorknob from him. "Are all your tenants so satisfied after their first night in your building?"

Luke chuckled and despite the dim light in the hall, Domino spied a blush creep up his neck. "You'll have to ask them."

If he only knew what questions she needed to ask. "I'll do that."

He pushed away from the doorjamb, then stopped and turned. "I left the week-to-week contract on the bed."

Which she'd already filled out and signed.

"Oh," she said, feigning surprise. "I'll get those to you later on, if that's okay."

"Works for me."

Wow. Domino had made love to a lot of men, but never once had she experienced a moment so incredibly…awkward. For the first time in years, she experienced a momentary overlap of what she wanted to say and what she should say for the sake of the case.

She opted to say nothing at all.

With a wink, she shut her door, locked it and leaned against the hard, cool wood. Taking in a deep breath, she listened as his footfalls retreated down the hallway. After the stairwell door creaked open and closed, she exhaled.

Instantly she clicked into agent mode. She retrieved

her duffel bag from the closet and extracted the security device she needed to ensure no one came into this apartment uninvited, or at least, undetected. With her eyes and fingers engaged in her work and her ears trained for any sign of someone approaching, she pulled apart the doorknob, inserted and attached the mechanism, tested the power source and finally put everything back together. Then she went back inside, locked the door behind her and stopped long enough to breathe.

Why was she shaking?

The sex. Mind-blowing, infinitely pleasurable, overload-the-senses sex. Had her cell phone not trilled with a series of musical notes identifying the caller as Darwin, she might have had more time to relive the sensations. Instead she jabbed the talk button with uncharacteristic impatience.

"Domino," she replied.

"Report."

"Area not secure," she admitted. She hadn't had time to install the jamming device that would render all listening apparatus useless within a one-mile radius of her room.

"What have you been doing all night?"

She didn't reply and knew Darwin didn't expect her to, not without all protocols in place. She disconnected, knowing he'd give her just enough time to do what should have been done hours ago before he called back. Just short of two minutes after she'd activated the last circuit, the phone trilled again.

"This is why I hate this kind of operation," she

groused. Listening devices, hidden cameras, searches and adhering to protocols. Life was entirely easier when her only goal was death.

"Report," Darwin repeated.

"I've located a small safe in Luke Brasco's bathroom, hidden under a loose tile."

"Contents?"

"Undetermined. I didn't have the right equipment to crack the code."

"When will you have another shot at it?"

Whenever I want another mind-blasting orgasm, I suppose.

"By tonight."

"Affirmative," Darwin replied, which was her handler's code-speak for "job well done."

"Anything else noteworthy in your search of his apartment?"

"He's definitely no techno-geek. He doesn't have a computer there. No iPod. No PDA. His stereo equipment is at least ten years old. Even his answering machine works on tape rather than on digital technology."

"Anything interesting on his messages?"

"Negative. So far as I could see, no one calls him at home. And all calls registered in his cell phone are clearly work-related."

Darwin paused and while he processed the information she'd given him, Domino indulged in a face-stretching, eye-watering yawn.

"Can you gain access to his club office?" Darwin asked.

"Affirmative. I'll report back when I get something."

"What's first on your agenda?"

Domino pulled the phone away from her ear. She fully expected to give Darwin play-by-plays once she'd completed certain tasks, but it had been years since she'd been asked to review her strategy ahead of time. She worked with Darwin and under his command, but for the most part once she was in the field, she operated on her own training and gut instinct, with very little to no interference beyond support. She supposed if she wanted to move up in The Shadow world, she'd better hone her team player skills. But tonight, she was too damned tired.

"My first priority is sleep," she replied, yawning again, this time without any pretense of covering her exhaustion.

"I take it that means you spent the night with Mr. Brasco?"

"That was the plan, wasn't it? I'll contact you again after I have something solid."

She flipped the phone closed and tossed it onto the bed, but couldn't help staring at it for a few moments longer, as if the slim communicator would somehow tell her if her curt tone had messed up her chances of parlaying this mission into a promotion within The Shadow. Fortunately she was too tired to care much beyond a few seconds of regret. For all she knew, the change in her assignment from assassin to investigator meant nothing except exactly what Darwin had initially said—they needed one agent and one agent only, in and out quickly and efficiently. Or it was more. She didn't know and until she had at least four hours of z's under her belt, she didn't care.

She collected all her materials, stuffed them in the duffel and shoved the whole lot in the closet before stripping out of her clothes and climbing into bed. With her security system in place, she took less than thirty seconds to fall blissfully into sleep, hoping, for an instant, that she'd dream of making love with Luke Brasco and not of killing him.

"SO WHO IS SHE?"

Luke hadn't even closed his door behind him when he heard his stepmother's voice reverberating off the narrow hallway walls. He took a deep breath and turned to face her, not really looking forward to this conversation, especially since it was three o'clock in the afternoon and he still hadn't had his first cup of coffee.

"Good to see you, too, Glo," he greeted with a backhanded yawn.

For some reason, his stepmother thought she should be consulted in all matters concerning the building and the club, including who came and went. Sure, she lived here and she'd fronted him some money way back in the beginning, but he'd paid her back, with interest, and once he'd turned twenty-five, the building ownership had been legally transferred to him.

Yet, he indulged her. She was, after all, the only family he had left, except for his half brother, Marcus, who for all intents and purposes, was out of both their lives for good. Luke had no desire ever to see the inside of a prison cell, or even the visitors' yard. Not when he'd warned his younger brother about dabbling in shit he didn't know about. Not when Luke had done everything within his limited power to keep Marcus from going down the wrong road.

"Done with inventory?"

She scowled at him. "Finished it yesterday and you damned well know it. So who is the chick staying in Mathers's old room?"

"Her name is Domino Black."

"Sounds like an alias."

"You watch too much television. I checked her out. She's a relatively well-known photographer who's in Chicago to work."

"She got a Web site?"

"Yes," he replied, though he hadn't gone online to verify that. Since his brother had screwed up so royally, Luke's aversion to computers meant he didn't have much interest in the World Wide Web. He'd only allowed Gloria to design and maintain a Web site for the club because it kept her out of his hair on the subject. His disc jockeys also used a complicated system to program the music, but Luke stayed away from that apparatus and most of the guys seemed relieved. The only technology he couldn't avoid using personally was the surveillance equipment. He did, in fact, have an old computer in his office but he never touched the thing.

"What's the URL?" Gloria asked.

URL?

"The Web address," she clarified.

He shook his head. "I don't know. Giggle her."

"That's Google, you moron."

"I love you, too, Glo. Anything you need me for? Because if I don't get to the kitchen soon and hook myself up with some seriously caffeinated coffee, I'm going to be a bear to work for later on."

"You're always a bear to work for."

To prove her right, he growled and bared his teeth before making his way downstairs. He found himself pausing on the second landing for a moment, long enough to wonder if Domino was as exhausted as he was, and if she'd enjoyed herself last night as much as he had—though he was fairly certain that she had since she hadn't been exactly quiet about her orgasmic responses. But before he could surrender to his instinct to tap on her door, or perhaps even use his master key to let himself in, Gloria jogged down the steps behind him and gave him a shove in the shoulder.

"Get moving, bossman. Some of us have work to do."

As gallantly as possible, he allowed her to pass him, then followed close behind. He needed to build a little distance between him and his new tenant. What did he really know about her, beyond the exact location of her clit and the precise amount of pressure he needed to push her instantly over the edge? In the light of the new day, he couldn't help but wonder what she might be hiding—what secrets she kept buried deep behind those cobalt-blue eyes.

All women had secrets. All men, too. No exceptions. None that he'd come across, anyway. And most of the time, those untold truths had the power to destroy relationships—even the least complicated ones. Even the ones based solely on hot, sweaty sex.

"SO, YOU'RE THE NEW GIRL?"

Domino had heard the footsteps behind her, but had made the conscious choice not to scurry out of sight. She'd had more than enough time to search the employee locker room and had come up empty. She intended to get back into Luke's room as soon as he decided to wake up and start his day.

She extended her hand to the brassy redhead in the impossibly tight blouse. "I'm Domino. Domino Black."

"Sienna Monroe."

Sienna? How cute. Her name matched her hair color. Not that Domino had that much room to talk, considering that her last name matched hers.

"Luke didn't say he was hiring a new waitress," Sienna said, folded her arms suspiciously across her abundant chest.

"I'm not a waitress," Domino explained. "I just moved into the apartment upstairs."

"What apartment? They're all taken."

"Some guy named Carson Mathers lit out, but gave me the lead on the space. I moved in last night."

Sienna narrowed her heavily made-up eyes. "If you have all that space up there, why are you snooping around down here?"

Because it's my job, you silicone-enhanced, postpubescent bimbo.

"Luke told me to look around," she replied, exhausting her most friendly grin. "I used to work in a joint just like this one in London. Or maybe it was Monte Carlo. I travel a lot. All the places eventually meld together."

The girl licked her lips, but refused to be impressed, judging by her stoic expression.

Too bad this bitch wasn't the traitor. Domino might just enjoy offing her. The woman gave off a seriously annoying vibe, but appeared too self-absorbed to be a double-crossing mastermind. Still, Domino would check her out just as she'd check out each and every one of Luke's employees. Maybe she'd get lucky.

But if this job had a downside, this was it. Ninety-nine percent of the time, she didn't interact with her targets. She felt nothing about killing them, not when she had thick dossiers detailing the threats the targets posed to national security or the atrocities her targets committed on their tiny island nation or within their South American cartel. For the first time that Domino could remember, she was interacting with people she might have to kill—except for this chick, obviously, who clearly didn't have the brainpower to figure out she shouldn't act like a brat to a woman who could snap her neck without breaking a sweat.

"Maybe you should travel back to one of those places," a female voice echoed from behind Sienna, who stepped aside with a nasty smile on her voice.

Great. What's worse than one sarcastic bitch? Two, clearly.

Domino stretched out her hand. "You must be Gloria."

The woman returned her smile, but with fake sincerity. At least this one had a tad more finesse.

"The one and only. And you're the chippie who's been distracting my son."

"Stepson," a male voice said.

The catty aura in the room was instantly squashed by Luke's potent male presence. Domino watched the scene shift with complete fascination. Sienna instantly darted out of the room. Gloria stood her ground, but her shoulders, so squared and primed for battle just moments before, now curved in subtle surrender.

"You know what I meant," Gloria capitulated.

Luke had the class to give her a smile. "Of course I did. But I also know you were about to be incredibly rude to my new tenant. You're going to be living down the hall from her, Glo. Don't you think you can manage to be a bit more welcoming?"

Gloria's eyes blazed, but her tongue remained in tight check, which was doing a real number on her jaw. "Got a weird vibe is all," she said by way of explanation.

Interesting.

Domino stepped forward and extended her hand again.

"As a photographer, I'm a natural observer. I watch everything around me and that tends to make people a little…nervous."

Of course, this was the first time Domino had interacted with Luke's stepmother. She might have figured that Gloria's overprotectiveness stemmed from natural parental concern, but Domino had read the dossier. Orphaned since age six, Luke hadn't had any choice but live with Gloria and grow up under her roof. But she wasn't exactly a nominee for mother of the year. No, the antagonism emanating from Gloria's keen stare and defensive stance came from another source—one Domino intended to discover.

Once Luke cleared his throat, Gloria finally accepted Domino's hand. The shake was curt, but seemed to satisfy all parties involved.

Gloria spun on Luke. "We still pushing the rum?"

He shook his head. Yes, back to business was much more comfortable. "Tonight it's the tequila."

Gloria acknowledged his decision and bustled out.

Domino licked her lips. "Mmm…tequila. I happen to love tequila."

He extended his hand to her, which she accepted, despite the unnerving coil of trepidation the gesture inspired. It was simple. Intimate. Natural. Most people wouldn't think twice about holding hands with a man they'd made love to just a few hours after the act. But most people weren't Domino Black.

He reeled her in against him and she couldn't help but lean into the warmth.

"I figured you for more of a vodka gal."

"Vodka?" she asked, exaggerating her offense. "How derivative. I've never drank a Cosmo in my life and I don't intend to start now."

He tugged her out of the employee locker area and, oddly, didn't ask her why she'd been there. "But a Margarita will do?"

"I prefer my tequila like I prefer my men—straight, strong and with a worm I can bite the head off of."

"I hope you mean that sexually and not figuratively," he joked.

She only arched a brow. "There's always literally."

He laughed heartily and Domino couldn't help but share the chuckle. Laughing with him was way too easy...and that scared her more than any terrorist ever would.

6

SIENNA SNAPPED HER APRON like a whip, accidentally flicking a votive candle so that it crashed off the table she was supposed to be readying for the club's opening.

"Damn!"

She dropped to the floor and amid a string of choice curses that only increased her anger, picked up the scattered pieces of broken glass. No big surprise when one of the slivers sliced into her finger. This time, she screamed her four-letter words at the top of her lungs.

"That's some potty mouth you've got."

Sienna spun to her left, ready to decimate whomever had the balls to criticize her when she was in pain, but her verbal assault jerked to a stop when she saw Mikey emerge from Luke's office, a wry smile on his roughly handsome face.

Instantly her insides melted into goo. Thick, hot, raspberry-flavored gelatinous goo, like the kind she'd like to smear all over the big guy's naked body and then lap up with her tongue. The sting and throbbing of her cut disappeared and all she could think about was that she finally had a chance to push good old married Mikey over the edge.

She'd stuck her finger in her mouth, but with as much sexiness as possible, she popped the digit out from between her lips and showed him the damage.

"Wanna kiss my boo-boo?"

He only arched a brow. Damn, but the man could be stubborn. Of course, maybe cutesy sex kitten wasn't the way to go. His wife certainly didn't fit that description. She was more the athletic, all-American type. Sienna supposed she'd been pretty enough before she'd ballooned to a size sixteen with the two buns in her oven. Under the circumstances, Sienna couldn't understand his resistance. She knew he wanted her. What was there not to want? She had a hot body, great tits and an ass that didn't quit. Okay, so the boy wore a wedding band and he had knocked up his wife, but that was all the more reason for him to dip his dick in a free and willing well that he didn't have to share with his soon-to-be rugrat.

"I'll get the first-aid kit."

She shrugged. Whatever. She would have thought it gross if he'd wanted to suck her blood anyway. She couldn't understand the whole vampire fantasy, not with STDs floating around the club scene like confetti on New Year's Eve.

Mikey returned from the office with a small white and blue box emblazoned with a red cross. He flipped the lid with confidence, extracted antibiotic ointment and a small adhesive bandage.

She had the finger back in her mouth, but he waved it out with an impatient glare.

"Do you know how many germs you have in your mouth?"

She scoffed at him, affronted. "Hello? I use the best mouthwash on the market," she said, leaning forward so she could blow her mint-scented breath across his face. "Or can't you tell?"

He recoiled, but completely without expression. He was fighting the vibe. She knew it.

"Yeah, well, give me the hand so I can clean this up."

He worked with quick efficiency, wiping the cut with an antiseptic wipe, smearing on a dollop of ointment and then securing a bandage with just enough tightness to keep it in place, but not enough to cut off her circulation. The man was good with his hands. God, why was he being so impervious to what she knew they both wanted?

"Where'd you learn to do that?" she asked breathlessly as he tidied up the mess around them, dumping the broken glass pieces into a pile on top of the table.

"Afghanistan."

She knew he'd been overseas in the military, but had no idea where he'd served. "You were a medic?"

"No," he replied. "Infantry. But when injuries are minor, there's no need to call a real doctor. You learn to handle shit yourself."

She snatched her hand back. First, she didn't like his dismissive tone. Second, she couldn't stand the overload to her senses caused by his touch—not when he was being so stingy about it. She considered insisting that her injury wasn't minor, but she wasn't stupid. The man had been at war. If she'd learned one thing growing up in a family that had more veterans than a war memorial, it was that you didn't earn brownie points by insulting a man's military service.

"Well, thanks," she said, hopping to her feet.

"Why were you so angry at the candle?"

Her ire intensified and she cast a glance over her shoulder. Luke was giving a personal tour of the club to the wench with the black hair and perfect boots. Who the hell did she think she was, anyway?

"I wasn't angry at the candle," she said through clenched teeth.

He chuckled. "I see you met Domino."

"Is that really her name?"

With a shrug, Mikey retrieved a tray from the top of the bar and slid the broken glass onto it. "Beats me. But she's with the boss, so you'd better be polite. Trust me." He rubbed his wrist, but Sienna didn't know why.

"I don't like her," she said, satisfied at finally voicing her opinion out loud. Again. Gloria, luckily, seemed to share her assessment that the new tenant was not to be trusted.

"I have a feeling most women don't," Mikey said with a chuckle.

"What is that supposed to mean?"

Mikey marched behind the bar and took his time disposing of the mess. He'd pursed his lips, as if wondering whether or not he wanted to continue this conversation with her. She hoped he did. So far, talking about the boss's new fuck-buddy had resulted in the longest conversation she'd had with Mikey since she decided she wanted to be his…well, fuck-buddy.

"How can I put this delicately?" he asked.

She shoved her hands onto her hips. "If you haven't noticed, I'm not delicate. Are you saying I'm jealous?"

"Aren't you?"

"Of what? Sure, she's attractive in an exotic, mysterious, foreign sort of way. What nationality is she, anyway?"

Again, he shrugged. Before Luke invited the chick into his office, Sienna tried to place her facial features, her coloring, her accent—but couldn't. She'd said she'd lived overseas. She was probably some glamorous world traveler who went to all kinds of exotic places and met all kinds of fascinating people. How could Sienna compete with that?

Only she didn't have to compete, did she? Yeah, she'd once considered making a move for the boss, but after working with him for a few days, she figured he was just too old for her. Not in years, but in attitude. She wanted someone she could tempt and seduce. Someone like Mikey. Not that she was doing such a bang-up job in the seduction department with him, but she was still getting warmed up.

"Gloria doesn't like her," Sienna said, hoping that was enough to explain her instantaneous dislike for Luke's new play toy. She wasn't buying that she was jealous. This Domino woman hadn't made a play for Mikey.

"Gloria doesn't like any woman who shows interest in Luke," Mikey pointed out. "Remember how rude she was to Cecily?"

"Cecily was before my time," she reminded him.

"Well, Gloria treated her like crap. After a while, Cecily wouldn't even come to the club anymore, and trust me, she could hold her own in nearly all situations.

But Gloria was relentless and Cecily decided it wasn't worth the shit to hang out here."

"Is that why she and Luke broke up?"

Mikey sneered. "Nah. I don't know why they split exactly, but Luke would never let his stepmother get in the way if he really loved a woman."

Sienna laughed, shook out her apron and wrapped it tightly around her waist. "I had no idea you were such a sappy romantic."

"Sappy?" he asked, his voice suddenly dipping low as his chest puffed up high. "I'm not sappy."

"Yes, you are!" She leaned sexily across the table and retrieved her wet rag. "No wonder you keep turning me down. I'm not exactly the type for roses and chocolates, am I? But I bet you get off on that shit, don't you? Seeing the little wifey get all hot and bothered over a five-dollar box of Whitman's."

Mikey's face reddened and for a moment, Sienna thought he might lash out at her. So far, he'd caged his denials of her freely offered affection with politeness. Maybe she'd pushed too far? In a way, she'd insulted his manhood just as she had his choice of spouse. She opened her mouth to rephrase her comment, but then changed her mind. Hey, if he wanted to screw around with her just to prove he was a man, she wouldn't complain.

Instead he walked away. He disappeared out the front door of the club and when she turned to resume her duties with the tables, she yelped, surprised at Domino's presence behind her.

"Where the hell did you come from?"

"The office," she answered coolly. "Luke had to take a call. Not having much luck with big Mikey there, are you?"

"You don't know what the hell you're talking about," Sienna seethed. She turned and went back to her work, scrubbing with more energy than necessary.

"Right. Okay, that's cool. Clearly you know he's married and you don't care. Or maybe that's what turns you on. Whatever. But he's obviously not interested. I don't know why a woman would waste her time."

Sienna slammed the rag down on the polished, but pocked surface of the table. "I'm not wasting anything. And it's none of your business, okay? You might be fucking the boss, but that doesn't give you free rein around here, got it?"

Domino put her hands up in mock surrender. "Message received. You have yourself a great day," she replied, her sarcasm dripping as she turned toward the back staircase.

Domino had only gotten under the girl's skin to get to know her better. Something about the lazy waitress had piqued her interest since their first meeting in the locker room. She seemed way too young, too naïve and too self-indulgent to be involved in the spy trade, but Domino couldn't be sure. Sienna Monroe seemed easily malleable. Just the kind of girl who could be made a stooge by someone with finesse and a sinister agenda.

On her way upstairs, Domino glanced back at the door to the club office, which was still firmly shut. At least she'd noticed one thing while inside—Luke had a computer. It wasn't state-of-the-art, but an Internet connection existed, as well as a few interesting peripherals, including a Webcam. When she had a chance, she'd see just what the man kept on his hard drive.

Once in her room, Domino extracted her laptop from her secured closet and keyed into the surveillance device she'd just left in the club office. Luke was still on the phone, but no longer with the dairy vendor who'd shorted them on a delivery of cheese they needed for the night's special—quesadillas. Instead he was talking to his accountant.

Domino set the device to record, programmed an earpiece to monitor the discussion at a low volume, grabbed her tool kit and proceeded upstairs.

She'd had the wax impressions converted to keys early this morning thanks to a mobile unit sent into the alley beneath her window. Darwin could pull out the stops when he needed to. With no one wandering around near the apartment, she entered Luke's domain with ease.

Daylight streamed in dusty columns through the windows and flickered off of a floor that needed a serious sweep. Clearly Luke Brasco wasn't the type to engage a housekeeper, nor was he prone to more than surface cleaning. He seemed incredibly private. That he'd allowed her into his room after knowing her for less than twenty-four hours seemed an utter contradiction if what The Shadow suspected about him was true. Which made her all the more curious about what Luke had placed in a secure safe underneath a bathroom tile.

His conversation with his accountant continued in her ear, filled with jovial laughter and references to

Luke's inability to join the rest of the world in the twenty-first century. She'd spied the old-fashioned ledgers on his desk. Coupled with what she'd discovered about his lack of technology in his personal life, the ledgers didn't surprise her, but they did concern her. The spy game today was fraught with coded messages and encrypted communication. Once again, she wondered if his backwater attitude toward gadgets was a fact that eliminated him as the spy or was a cover to throw suspicion off him.

But even the safe underneath the tile was the old-fashioned kind with tumblers and pins. Old-fashioned. Old school. As such, she dispensed with the lock in less than a minute.

Inside was a folded-up stack of papers.

She adjusted the earpiece. Luke was chitchatting with his accountant about the Cubs having a shot at the World Series. She unfolded the papers. Computer printouts. Her eyes darted over the information and she found herself holding her breath until her chest ached. She grabbed her encrypted cell phone from her pocket and pressed the button that would connect her to Darwin.

"Report," he said as a hello.

"I've retrieved the contents of Luke Brasco's safe."

"And they are?"

Domino swallowed hard. The information looked outdated. At least five years old judging by the time stamps in the corner. But the contents couldn't be disputed.

"Computer printouts," she replied.

"From?"

"The Pentagon."

LUKE HUNG UP THE PHONE and instantly wondered where Domino had disappeared to. He no longer fought the fact that she popped into his mind at random moments, opportune or not. For now, he could manage to go with the flow. Why fight it? He wandered into the club, which was empty, though sounds from the kitchen rattled and clanked, and from the storeroom he could hear the shuffle of boxes and booze. He checked his watch. At least five hours until the biggest crowds descended and as always, Club Cicero would be more than prepared. Tonight, the club sported a *Cinco de Mayo* theme, even though the real holiday was months away. Sienna had already cleared and sct up all the tables with votive candles in the bright colors of the Mexican flag and the cleaning crew, on duty before sunrise, had done a more than decent job on the floor and walls. For at least the first few minutes after opening, the place would gleam and glitter. He'd scheduled a live band from California that played a raucous mix of techno Tejano music and he'd stocked up on salt, lime and tequila for the body shots he was sure would ensue. Tonight would be wild and unpredictable—and the take at the door would surely placate his nervous accountant. So a few numbers didn't quite add up, even after close scrutiny. They'd find the discrepancy. They always did.

He couldn't let this financial hiccup overtake his

life right now. Under normal circumstances, he'd have bundled the ledgers and receipts and parked his butt on his accountant's doorstep until they found every last penny. But it was only a couple of thousand that was unaccounted for and tonight, he had more important things on his mind.

Domino.

Every jaded fiber of his body wanted to push her aside in favor of concentrating on Club Cicero, but he couldn't get her out of his mind. Their lovemaking had been unbelievable. Notwithstanding the weird headache he'd woken up with halfway through the night, he couldn't remember ever feeling so at ease, and yet, at the same time, so deliciously tense, with a brand-new woman. She'd exceeded every expectation he'd ever had for a lover and for the first time in a long while, he wondered, only for a second, if he'd measured up to her standard.

If someone had asked him to detail the qualities of his fantasy woman, he would have described Domino point for point. Her hair color. Her eye color. Her panther tattoo. Her sharp tongue, naughty streak and mysterious quality. Even her chosen career fit with his idea of an ideal woman—professional and artistic, yet flexible. She made her own hours, followed her own rules. A man like him—one without the need for permanent entanglements—had nothing to object to.

And yet, something niggled at him, an uncertain feeling fed by his natural inclination toward distrust. Hell, he'd only known her for a day. She was a stranger.

A puzzle. A present best unwrapped slowly, layer by layer, until he reached the prize within.

Three of his servers came into the main room, boxes of colorful decorations spilling over the sides. Luke gave them a nod. They needed no direction. Club Cicero hosted a Mexican themed night on the fifth of every month, one of the many alternate theme nights he'd instituted to make sure that the perennial gangster/speakeasy theme didn't grow old or stale.

God, he loved this place. The seediness. The raw displays. The camaraderie and endless pursuit of pleasure and fun. The nod to the past in tandem with the party club atmosphere of the here and now. And in a wave of emotion that surprised him, he couldn't wait to share the experience tonight, with Domino.

He turned to seek her out upstairs when Mikey marched in to the club, a scowl darkening his face. He kicked a bar stool out of his way, unaware that Luke was standing there until he cleared his throat.

"Don't tell me," Luke offered. "The entire security staff called in sick."

Mikey stopped, took a deep breath and released the air slowly. "Nothing so easy, boss."

The three servers throwing streamers across the outer wall burst into a fit of giggles, making Mikey tense even more.

Oh. Luke speculated that only one thing unnerved Mikey this much. Sienna. She wasn't among the decorators, but it took Mikey a few tense moments to figure that out. When he did, his shoulder muscles stopped their attack on his neck.

"You've got to put a stop to that crap, Mikey," Luke told him, as a friend, not a boss, though he figured Mikey wouldn't recognize the distinction. "You're leading her on."

"I am not!" his bouncer insisted. "I can't *not* talk to her. Unless you want to fire her."

Sienna could be lazy and was often annoying since she didn't know when to turn off the sexy vixen act she liked to play, but the customers loved her and so long as she was carrying her weight and bringing in tips, Luke couldn't dismiss her simply because she had a crush on his married chief of security.

"No can do. This is a personal matter between the two of you. Handle it. And don't," Luke said, pointing his finger at Mikey's chest, "let it disrupt business."

He wanted to give the guy more advice, show a little compassion, but really, who the hell was he to talk? He was having wild sex and blowing off business concerns because of a too-good-to-be-true woman he'd known for less than twenty-four hours. If he had any brains, he'd keep his sage wisdom to himself. Mikey was a big boy in more than just the physical sense. If he wanted to jeopardize his marriage and family because some dish was hot for him, what could Luke do? The bottom line was, if Mikey hadn't been sending mixed messages, Sienna would have already moved on to someone else. It was how things worked.

After discussing a few more details with Mikey regarding the crowd tonight since they were hosting a live band rather than just a disc jockey, Luke checked in with the kitchen, had a brief meeting with Gloria and her bar staff, then headed upstairs for a late lunch. He entered his apartment and for a split second, thought he could smell the distinct scent of Domino's perfume. Hadn't been that long since she left, now that he thought about it. And smelling her was definitely better than whiffing the odor of old hot dogs.

Opting to make a culinary change, he dialed the number of the Chinese place down the street, but clicked the receiver down before they answered. Maybe Domino was hungry. They could talk over dim sum. Get to know each other in more than just the physical sense. Or, even better, they could talk, eat and then have some more hot sex before the club opened.

Unfortunately, when he knocked on her door, there was no answer. She did have a photo assignment to pursue. She couldn't be at his sexual beck and call every moment of the day. Well, yeah, she could, he thought with a smile. Alas, his fantasy woman was becoming more and more real—and the worst part was, he didn't really mind.

THE BAND HAD SHIFTED into high gear. Domino felt the floor pulse with the intense Tejano beat long before she reached the main floor. She slipped through the hall that separated the club from the stairwell to the rooms upstairs and gave a curt nod to the security guard—Craig, if she remembered correctly—posted by the door.

The atmosphere in the club was entirely different than the night before. The music. The decorations. The margaritas. She spied a few couples doing body shots at the bar and considered taking part. That ought to rattle Luke Brasco a bit. But she didn't need him rattled at the moment. She needed him preoccupied.

Which was why The Shadow had two agents making a fuss at the club entrance at this very moment. The minute Domino's surveillance device showed him darting outside his office to help out his security staff at the front door, leaving his desk and computer abandoned, she'd snuck out of her room. She'd considered waiting to do her recognizance after the club had closed for the night, but time was of the essence in this case. The Pentagon printouts she'd found in Luke's safe detailing the arsenal inventory for several bases in Bahrain, Kuwait and Yemen might have been outdated and completely unrelated to the identities of embedded agents, but the manifests proved Lucas Brasco had ties to someone with inside connections. The proof wasn't strong enough to guarantee a death warrant, but suspicion had now been raised to dangerous levels. Domino's discovery had moved Luke Brasco one step closer to elimination—and she was trying her damnedest not to think about how that made her feel.

How she felt didn't matter. Had never mattered. She had a job to do. A career to advance. A life to possibly, someday, lead fully and openly, without being relegated to the deepest, darkest shadows of covert operations. A chance to move up.

To move on.

She eased through the crowd, making no eye contact. When she was a few feet away from the office door and the couple making out nearby dashed onto the dance floor, she made her move. With a flick of a switch attached to her watch, she activated a device she'd placed earlier on the main power source to the club. The lights flickered. The music drained out of the speakers. Two seconds later, the club went entirely black. By the time she'd slipped inside, the lights flashed back on and the screams of surprise died down and melded back into the expected club din.

She had to work quickly.

"I'm in," she said, knowing Darwin had patched in at her request to act as her lookout.

"Affirmative. Brasco is still outside. Proceed."

She was already at the computer. Surprisingly the unit was turned on and she only needed a few minutes to bypass his passwords. She inserted a special USB device into the port and began the process of downloading the contents of his hard drive. In the meantime, she did a quick check of his desk and couldn't help but notice, again, the old-fashioned ledgers.

"Have you checked Brasco's financials lately?" she asked Darwin.

His disembodied voice whispered, "he made a phone call to his accountant today that indicated a discrepancy in his account of five thousand dollars. He set up a meeting to go over the numbers tomorrow."

"Five thousand doesn't sound like much," she said as she skimmed through the employee files.

"It's not, but if Brasco is experiencing financial trouble we haven't yet picked up on, he could have a motive for betraying his country. We're checking further."

Out of morbid curiosity, Domino pulled out Sienna

Monroe's file. "What have you got on Sienna Monroe, born January 22, 1985?"

She could hear brisk typing on the other end of the connection. "I have nothing for a Sienna Monroe born on that date."

Odd. She flipped through the papers and found her tax records. "Wait. Try Anne—with an e—Sienna Monroe. Same birth date."

More keyboarding.

"That's interesting," Darwin intoned.

Domino stopped rummaging. "What's interesting?"

"Anne Sienna Monroe is the niece of Senator Paul Monroe."

Since Domino spent so much time out of the country, she didn't know the names of the political players in Washington—at least, not beyond the big guys like the president and speaker of the house.

"And he is?"

"Democratic senator from California."

Meant nothing.

"So why is this interesting?"

"He's vice chairman of the Select Committee on Intelligence."

Ah. "Then he could have access to the names of our agents."

She stuffed the files back into place, intrigued by this turn of events. She'd figured Sienna as no more than an oversexed pain in the ass. Could she be, at the very least, the source of the agent identities? Maybe working with Luke? As a coconspirator, he'd need to keep her around, despite her marginal waitressing skills and annoying personality.

"I'm forwarding this information to an agent on the inside in Congress," Darwin reported. "Keep an eye on her and don't make a move against Brasco until we follow this lead."

Domino didn't realize she'd expelled a sigh of relief until her chest lightened.

"Do you mean I shouldn't make a move in the official sense, or in the personal one?" she joked.

Darwin didn't reply to her clearly rhetorical question, but instead reported that according to the surveillance cameras, Luke had handled the situation outside and would soon return inside the club. With quick efficiency, Domino tidied the office to its original state. She hadn't completed the search, but she'd return after hours to check out whatever she might have missed. After retrieving her portable USB drive and erasing all proof of her download from the computer, she prepared to leave.

She moved to activate the power surge device again when the door swung open.

"Aha!" Gloria shouted, rushing in and grabbing Domino by the hair and yanking hard. "I knew I'd find you up to no good!"

Domino executed a quick twist. Gloria held fast to her hair, but in seconds, Domino had the woman snared in front of her with her arm twisted behind her back and Domino's hand clutched to the woman's windpipe.

"You just made a fatal error, stepmother," she said, hissing into the woman's ear.

But she didn't have time to finish what Gloria had so woefully started. First, there was the matter of Darwin shouting in her ear for her to stand down. And second there was Luke standing breathless in the doorway, all blood drained from his face.

7

"WHAT'S GOING ON HERE?"

Luke gaped, completely immobilized by the scene in front of him. His lover was holding his stepmother in an effective and painful looking chokehold. She'd barely broken a sweat even though Gloria had a life-grip on her long, black hair. After a few seconds, Domino loosened her hold enough to allow Gloria to scream.

"Get her off me!" Gloria rasped. "Luke, she was in here. Snooping around. Trying to rob you blind!"

Domino's eyes, so blue and expressive and warm only hours before, now gleamed with hard coldness. She held Gloria steady despite the woman's continued attempts to yank her hair out by the roots.

"Calm down and I'll release you," Domino said.

Her tone sent a shiver up Luke's spine. Flat. Emotionless. And dead serious.

Gloria renewed her screams, nearly shattering Luke's eardrums. He rushed forward and grabbed his stepmother by the shoulders.

"Gloria, let go of her hair!" he ordered.

His stepmother cursed a blue streak, but obeyed.

The minute she disentangled her fingers, Domino stepped back and raised her arms in surrender.

Instantly Gloria launched into a high-pitched rant, spinning on Domino, but Luke held her as still as he could manage. Despite the music and laughter and general deafening noise in the club, he dragged her with him to close the door, bracing her with his hands as he tried to pacify her. Behind them, Domino leaned back against a filing cabinet, crossed her arms over her chest and rolled her eyes at the ceiling.

"Glo, calm down. I'm not listening to a thing you have to say until you're rational."

Panting heavily, Gloria forced huge gulps of air into her lungs and shrugged out of Luke's hold. She patted her hair back into place and then spun to face Domino. "You snuck in here! I saw you from across the bar. Didn't know I was watching you, did you, girlie? I won't have you coming in here and taking advantage of Luke! He doesn't need the kind of trash you're peddling."

Domino remained silent, an almost bored expression on her face. When it became clear she wasn't planning to respond to Gloria's accusations, Luke took a step closer.

"Did you break into my office?" he asked her.

"If coming in here to wait for you is considered breaking in, then, yes, I'm guilty as charged." She held out her wrists. "Want to cuff me?"

She winked. And despite the gravity of the situation, his dick hardened. First blindfolds and now handcuffs? He was turning into a real sexual deviant.

"Why'd the lights go out right before you came

inside, huh?" Gloria shouted, interrupting the banter. "Ask her that, Luke! Ask her."

Luke took a deep breath. Gloria had always been high-strung, but she'd never exhibited paranoia quite like this before. Why did she care if Domino came into the office unaccompanied? What could she steal except some old computer equipment and personnel files? The night's receipts were dumped at regular intervals into a floor safe with a timed lock. No one would be able to access the club's take until morning, when the Brinks guy showed up to make his run to the bank.

Luke leveled a patient look at Domino and hoped she read his unspoken plea to humor Gloria long enough to get her back behind the bar.

"My magnetic personality?" she asked, her cadence clearly indicating that the true explanation was obvious. A short in the wiring. Wouldn't be the first time or the last. "Look, I don't know anything about your electric system. I came to the office to look for you since I've been gone all afternoon. You weren't here, but since you told me you had some paperwork to go over tonight, I figured you'd be back. So I waited."

Her explanation was entirely reasonable, her tone level and calm. He'd pegged her for a cool operator the first moment he'd seen her—now, his assessment reached a new level. If she could survive Gloria at her worst without losing her temper, Domino Black had to have a cooling unit attached to her veins.

He turned Gloria around gently. "Glo, that sounds like a reasonable explanation. Do you think, maybe, that you overreacted?"

Gloria glared at him, like venom spewing from her eye sockets. "She's a bad one, Luke. You don't think I know one when I see one?"

Luke smiled indulgently. "How could you, Glo? Underneath that rough exterior, you're a pussycat. I appreciate your maternal instincts kicking in again, but you're jumping to conclusions when you have no proof."

Gloria glanced over her shoulder at Domino, who luckily hadn't changed her passive expression. With nothing more to spur her on, Gloria slammed out of the office. If she was cursing or muttering on her way out, Luke couldn't hear her—which was fine, because he didn't want to.

He slipped his hands into the pockets of his khakis. "Sorry about that."

Finally Domino grinned.

"Your stepmother is insane, you know that, right?"

He tamped down a full-fledged smile. Gloria might be…eccentric…but she usually meant well. "I think she's trying to make up for all those nights she left me and my brother to our own devices while she went club-hopping with her girlfriends."

Domino pushed off the file cabinet and stalked toward him slowly. As if someone had dropped a veil across her face, her expression softened and the heat missing from her eyes moments before now flamed back to life.

"There's another one at home like you?" she asked.

Luke tried not to tense. Marcus was nothing like him. Nothing. He'd spent the last ten years trying to prove as much, if only to himself.

"Marcus left the nest a long time ago."

Domino glanced at the door through which Gloria had just exited. "I can't imagine why," she said, her sarcasm crisp.

"Gloria had her hands full with the two of us. I guess she did the best she could."

Finally near enough so that Luke could inhale the spicy scent of her perfume, Domino slid her hands up his chest, pressing her palms on his pectoral muscles. He knew she could feel his heartbeat. Either that, or the bass pulse from the band on the other side of the wall was striking straight through him. His entire body tensed with delicious tightness when she licked her lips and then, licked his.

"What do you say we stop talking about your stepmother?" she suggested.

"Sounds like an excellent plan," he replied, his voice thick and raspy.

She glanced speculatively at the door. "That sucker have a lock?"

Driven by her subtle suggestion, Luke went to the door and locked out the world. He really should have checked to make sure Gloria hadn't set the storeroom on fire in her wrath, but the minute his eyes met Domino's, all thoughts of his responsibilities oozed out of his body. Alone in his office—which suddenly seemed sensually dark, compact and intimate when normally, he saw it as dusty and closetlike—the lust he'd been holding in check while he tried to deal with the normal day-to-day operation of the club shot to the surface. In an instant, he had his hands locked behind her neck as he yanked her into a hot, wet, insistent kiss.

She responded instantly, tugging at his buttons until they popped free. She tore the material aside and he reveled in the feel of her hands and lips skimming his chest, sides, hips and waist with urgent need. Just above his nipples, she grabbed hold of his chest hair and pulled. The pain smarted just as it invigorated. He wanted her naked. Now.

He undid her jeans, but of course, the snug material wasn't going anywhere without her cooperation. She laughed, stepped back and shimmied out of the tight denim. When she hooked her arms around her to undo her blouse, he stopped her by grabbing her wrist.

"Oh, no…this is my job."

The halter top she wore had a buttoned closure just at the back of her neck and a zipper below her bared back. Whispering in her ear, he instructed her to lift her hair off her nape.

She complied. Luke pressed his hard body against her from behind, breathing deeply, inhaling the sweetness of her hair and skin. He flicked open the tiny snaps, then kissed a path down her spine before he undid the zipper and allowed the top to drift to the ground.

Her panties rode low on her hips, giving him an unhampered view of the tattoo that had nearly driven him insane when they'd first met. Tonight, he realized how much like the panther she was. Dark. Sleek. Mysterious. A huntress in every sense of the word. Had he invited an unknown danger into his life?

If he had, he didn't care. He wanted nothing more than to plunge into the peril. He dropped to his knees and slipped his hands beneath the thin straps of her thong, then tugged down until she was completely naked.

The curve of her bottom felt soft and hot against his mouth. The scent of her juices stirred him to madness. With his hands on her hips, he spun her around. She hooked one thigh over his shoulder and speared her hands into his hair, urging him to taste her until he had his fill.

He buoyed her with his hands and savored her textures and flavors until she cried out his name. Kissing, licking and lapping, he brought her to full orgasm, her muscles quivering and her balance faltering. But still he didn't stop. He had no desire to release his sensual hold on her. He continued to taste and explore until her need renewed. Her bruised flesh sweetened beneath his tongue and by the time she tugged him to stand, he knew he couldn't wait much longer to drive inside her. Luckily impatience drove her as well.

With an insistent push, she flattened him against his desk and removed his jeans. His sex jutted hard and hot and she took him into her mouth like a woman possessed. She held nothing back, but sucked until he was blind with need. He reached helplessly for his discarded jeans, muttering something about protection that made no sense, even to his own ears.

She winked at him, her intentions wicked. "Looking for this?" she asked, holding the condom between her fingers.

Thankfully she didn't need his response. She sheathed him, then with a tug on his arms, pulled him off the desk and switched places with him, her hand wrapped around his dick, stroking, toying, arousing.

She drew him to her, touching the tip of his head to her sex.

"All this hardness is turning me on," she breathed. "You, the desk…you."

He rubbed her smooth thighs, then up her body to the sweet curves of her breasts. Her flesh was moist and hot beneath his touch and he couldn't deny his need to press deep inside her, then slide out, then in. When she shifted and clutched her hands on the edge of the desk, creating the perfect brace for his movements, he thought he might lose his mind.

He didn't need her to urge him to thrust harder and faster, but hearing her deep, guttural commands spurred him. When she lifted one foot onto the table, shifting her body so that he could drive even deeper, he groaned in satisfaction. Then she moved her other foot. He buried his face in her shoulder as she clutched at his back, knowing he was driving right into her center by the way she cried out his name.

For a series of sparkling kaleidoscope moments Domino forgot who she was. Why she was here. What she was doing. She ceased being a Shadow agent manipulating a seduction and morphed into a woman solely giving and receiving pleasure.

She clutched at Luke's back, digging her nails into his smooth, musky skin. She couldn't seem to stop kissing him, tasting him, her lips addicted to the flavors of his shoulders, neck and mouth. The sound of his pleasured moans connected to something deep inside her that she didn't question, couldn't explain. She wanted more. She wanted to feel more. She wanted to taste more. She wanted to hear more. All from him. All right here, right now.

But neither of them could stop the momentum of their lovemaking and too soon, they were teetering on the precipice. Then he drove in one last time, filling her, pressing the precise spot that sent her flying into a fit of delicious quivering. Full, loud orgasms rocked both of them to the core. His sex slowly slackened inside her. And yet, she continued to shake.

"You…okay?" he asked, breathless.

For a long moment, she couldn't reply. She didn't have the brain capacity to form the words. She didn't have the muscle control to demand her tongue and lips and voice work in unison and reply to his question. It took her a full minute to regain her ability to even move out of his way and lower herself from the desk.

She grabbed her clothes from the floor and dressed as quickly as her trembling muscles allowed. Only once she was covered did she sweep her hand through her hair and catch sight of him staring at her with dark concern.

"What's wrong?"

"Wrong?" she asked, echoing the word. Wrong? Everything, damn it. Abso-fucking-lutely everything.

She forced a smile. "Let's not overanalyze this, handsome. You plain wore me out."

His grin cracked his face into two gorgeous halves. She marveled at how the physical exertion of their lovemaking had brought color high into his face, how his dilated pupils seemed a deeper, darker blue. She wondered how the thin sheen of perspiration coating his body would feel under her slick hands, which she shoved into her back pockets.

"I gotta go," she said, turning and placing her hand on the doorknob, spurring him to jump into his slacks in a way that was both clumsy and endearing.

She caught his worried expression, but made no move to alleviate his discomfort. She had her own crap to worry about right this minute, all thanks to him. So with a wink and a pause long enough for him to punch his arms into the sleeves of his shirt, she exited and made quick work of getting upstairs before anyone, most of all Gloria, waylaid her.

In the hall outside her room, she pressed the button on her watch to disable the alarm on her door and slipped inside as quickly as possible. She worked the locks, reactivated the security system and then stood with her forehead pressed against the hard wood. Her breath came in quick pants. Her heart sped in her chest so that she had to close her eyes to keep dizziness from overcoming her. Nausea swam in her stomach.

What the hell had just happened?

For a split second, she'd forgotten her purpose. She'd allowed sexual ecstasy to break through walls she'd worked fifteen years to build. The best defensive move she'd ever learned was to keep her emotions tightly controlled, protected by a layer of professional distance. How could she allow herself to open up or let people in when she knew she'd be gone soon, off on another assignment, deep in an underworld that could result in death?

She hadn't let Luke in, but her façade had cracked. She'd felt it and the resulting rush of emotion might have blown her away if she hadn't executed a narrow escape.

"I see I got here just in time."

She swung around, grabbed her gun from her stash by the door and aimed.

Darwin's arched brow forced her to stand down.

"What are you doing here?"

He put down the knickknack left in the room by some former tenant and faced her squarely. "That was some scene down there."

"Gloria Brasco is nuts."

"Gloria Brasco nearly caught you with your pants down."

She crossed her arms tight, hoping the gesture might help her control her rising temper. "That happened afterward, or weren't you watching?"

The corners of Darwin's mouth tilted downward. "I had the decency to disconnect from the feed before things…progressed."

"Why? Wasn't my fucking him part of the job? Or do you just not like to watch?"

Darwin's gaze narrowed. "Do you have a problem, Agent Black? I thought sleeping with the suspect was a dirty job you more than looked forward to."

"Fuck you."

"Either your vocabulary has shriveled or you're dealing with serious anger issues. I suggest you calm down."

She opened her mouth to suggest this time that he go fuck himself, but realized he wasn't off target. She was no prude, but since making love to Luke in his office, the four-letter epithet for the sexual act was rushing out of her mouth like vomit. She stepped back, closed her eyes and concentrated on regaining control. This wasn't like her. She didn't get involved. She didn't allow her emotions to push her to the limits or to rule her in any way. Thankfully, she had emotions. Never had she wanted to become a coldhearted, automaton of a killer who excelled as an assassin because she didn't give a damn about life. Her success stemmed from her belief that taking out threats to the United States government and its people was a necessary response. She was, through no fault of her own, especially suited for the missions. She'd had nothing to lose when she'd first come under the control of The Shadow. And for the first time since they'd popped her out of juvie and offered her the world in return for her soul, she was looking forward to more than simple existence. She saw the possibility of her own life to live. To control.

All at the expense of Luke Brasco.

"Why are you here?" she asked, calmly opening her eyes. "You're risking my cover. You could tip off our seller."

Darwin snorted. "I may not have been in the field much lately, but I can still do the job. I wanted to get an insider's view of the place and I had to bring you this."

He pulled a small memory card out of his pocket, which she snatched and examined. "For the camera?"

"In case someone wonders where all your photographs of Chicago are."

She disconnected the closet alarm and stored the card in her camera case. Having her back turned to Darwin gave her a few moments to regain her composure, at least temporarily. Claustrophobia suddenly threatened, a condition she'd never suffered from in her entire life. She figured the sensation of walls closing in and ceilings dropping had very little to do with a diagnosable mental disorder and everything to do with Luke Brasco.

"Any new reports on the buyer?" she asked.

"He's in the States."

"In Chicago?"

"Not yet. If our source is anywhere near accurate, he's part of a delegation from a small province in India currently attending a think-tank event in Washington, D.C."

"India?" she asked, surprised. So far as she knew, that country had very little stake in the information being brokered.

"Smoke screen," Darwin explained. "Several delegates have false papers. We're trying to sort out who is who."

"So you've detained them?"

Darwin shook his head. "We don't want to disrupt the operation. With you on the inside here and the potential buyers under surveillance, we should be able to avert any information leaking out. We're counting on you, Domino. We can't afford to have you distracted."

She narrowed her gaze at him, realizing for the first

time that she could take a great deal of pleasure in whacking her handler across the face.

"Don't you think you should make up your mind?" she asked. "Do you want me watching the club for a potential exchange or do you want me investigating Luke Brasco and figuring out if he's our mole?"

Darwin leaned back against the dresser, his hands slung into his pockets. "Maybe you were right. Maybe you're not cut out for this sort of work."

She stalked across the room and poked him hard in the chest as she spoke. "I can take whatever you want to dish out, got it? But I can only work with what I'm given. You keep an eye on that delegation and let me know if and when they arrive in Chicago. One way or another, the names of our agents will not fall into enemy hands."

Darwin looked entirely nonplussed.

"I've never doubted you," he said evenly.

She scoffed.

Darwin moved toward the exit. She gasped when her door opened. A Shadow agent, replete with dark suit and glasses, stood on the other side.

Holy shit. Had she gone upstairs so distracted that she not only hadn't noticed that Darwin had entered her room ahead of her, but also hadn't detected an agent watching from the hall? The agent had just bypassed her security without her hearing a sound? She had to get her shit together before she got herself killed—or, even worse, got herself discovered by the very information-mation broker they were trying to catch.

"What about the printouts?" she asked, her voice oddly shaky as she tried to recover her focus.

"As you suspected," he said after speaking softly to the agent and then closing the door again, "the information was old, but still highly classified. The techs are cross-checking to see if any damage has been caused by the release of that information to foreign sources, but we don't anticipate it has. Looks like simple manifests."

"But why would Luke have them?" she asked, more to herself than to Darwin.

He did not to reply. "We did check deeper into Sienna Monroe. Her bank accounts reflect a student slash waitress's income. She's not particularly close to her family and likely hasn't seen her uncle since her high school graduation."

"A dead end then?" she asked, only slightly disappointed. She didn't figure Sienna had the brains to pull off anything as complicated as selling state secrets, but she was clearly naïve and insecure enough to be manipulated by someone else. And quite frankly, Domino had taken a strong and insistent dislike to the twit. She would have felt no regret in removing her from the gene pool.

"More than likely. Concentrate on Brasco. He's still our best bet."

"What about his brother?" The question popped out of her mouth. When Luke had mentioned him tonight, his tone had been cold. Bad blood existed between the two, that much she could figure out. But why? Just because he was doing time in a federal pen for embezzlement?

"What about him?"

"He's in prison for stealing money, but could he also be into stealing government secrets?"

Darwin pursed his lips. "The information I reviewed while preparing the dossier showed him to have stolen over a million dollars from a software firm he was working for. He was caught, pleaded guilty and went to jail. Two years ago, he was transferred to a medium security facility. Luke never visits him and, as far as our records indicate, always refuses his phone calls."

"Does Gloria visit him?"

"Once a year before the holidays, maybe a few other times throughout the year. Typical maternal visitation."

"Does she talk to him on the phone?"

"Weekly."

"You've monitored the calls."

Darwin nodded. "Of course."

Domino didn't need to ask if they'd heard anything significant—if they had, she'd know. Still, she figured a little extra digging might not be a complete waste of time. "I want access to the brother's records. Transcripts."

"Whatever you need. The Committee has been exceedingly pleased with your progress. I do hope your personal interests don't change their opinion."

She narrowed her gaze at him, her anger shooting to the surface of her skin so that she figured she'd glow like nuclear waste if someone looked at her through heat-seeking binoculars. But she kept her rage in check. She trusted Darwin and his team, but she also trusted her own instincts. And if she wanted to explore every aspect of Luke Brasco's life before she marked him for death, that was her prerogative.

In fact, it was her job.

Darwin exited and the minute The Shadow agent

shut the door, Domino dashed forward and reactivated her so-called security system, cursing as she worked. She couldn't very well take herself to task for Darwin getting in—he had, after all, given her the codes. But damn it, she felt invaded from all directions and she had no one to blame but herself.

She yanked her laptop out from under the bed and typed her way into the ultrasecure Shadow network. If she couldn't find answers to the questions her emotions were bringing to bear, at least she could work on the case. Because, bottom line, she couldn't sort through anything personal until she knew for sure whether Luke Brasco was going to end up dead or alive.

8

LUKE FINISHED DRESSING and started to head back into the club when something stopped him. He glanced across the crowded dance floor and caught Gloria glaring at him from the other side of the bar. His stepmother could be an eccentric pain in the ass, but she was also, usually, a keen judge of character. To say she'd been around the block was a lot like saying John Glenn had taken a few interesting day trips. But judging by the way she'd once treated his former fiancée, Gloria's opinion of the women in his life couldn't always be trusted.

Still…

On a hunch that made his stomach roil with sickening anxiety, he returned to his office, shut the door, turned on all the lights and took a hard, long look around.

Trouble was, Luke wasn't one to pay diligent attention to little details. Had the ledgers been stacked neatly on top of each other or had he left them in a haphazard bundle? Had sex on the desk moved the position of the computer keyboard or had Domino been snooping around as Gloria suspected? And if she had been snooping, what of it? He couldn't fault her for curiosity. She was, after all, sleeping with a relative stranger.

He imagined that if she let him into her room upstairs—or if he lacked simple ethics and decided to use the master key when she was out—he'd want to dig a little deeper, find out what he could about her by the things left scattered on her dresser or by the clothing that hung in her closet.

The door opened behind him and he was relieved to see it was Mikey, entering as quietly as his hulking body would allow.

"Weird shit, boss."

"What?" Luke asked.

"That couple causing the ruckus up front."

Just about every night they had a nut job or two launch into some kind of rant, usually on account of the long lines leading into the club, the high cover charge or the refusal of his security staff to accept the laughable bribes they offered for immediate entrance into the club. Luke didn't figure tonight was any different. The couple certainly wasn't. Rich. Entitled. New to town. Same old, same old.

"Nothing you couldn't handle," Luke said.

Mikey smirked. "Then why did you come up front?"

"You asked me to, remember? I'm sure if left to your own devices, you would have controlled them. Eventually."

"Ha! They wouldn't even look me in the eye. Had to speak directly to the 'owner of the club,'" he said in full haughty imitation.

Luke just shrugged. Such crap was the downside of running a successful business.

He glanced at the ledgers. *One* of the downsides, he clarified.

He shuffled around the office a few minutes more and considered logging on to the computer to see if anyone—meaning Domino—had messed with anything, but he wouldn't have known the difference one way or another. Entirely by his choice, his computer knowledge was limited to e-mail. And even then, he didn't check his personal account more than once a week. Gloria handled answering all the business inquiries, so for the most part, his e-mail contained little but Nigerian scams and advertisements for natural male enhancement that Luke didn't need, thank you very much.

"I'm done in here," Luke said, grabbing the ledgers. He had to deliver them to the accountant in the morning. Might as well take them up to the apartment now. "How's the crowd?"

"Hot as ever."

"And the tequila?"

"Supply is holding up, but you'll have to put in a big order in the morning."

Luke and Mikey continued talking shop as he made his way through the club. So much easier to deal with the day-to-day operation of his business than contend with what had transpired between him and Domino. For twenty-four hours, he'd believed he'd finally found the one woman who appealed to every aspect of his most secret fantasies, not only physically, but emotionally. He needed a woman who was strong, sure of herself, capable of handling her own life separate and apart from his. Thanks to his upbringing with Gloria, he'd never excelled at taking care of other people beyond the basics. He'd figured Domino for the ultimate independent woman. Yet, despite her denial, Luke knew she'd left the office on a wave of fear.

The question was—fear of what? Of him? Of what he'd made her feel? Of what he was starting to feel for her?

Or of the consequences of being caught nosing around where she didn't belong?

THE TRILL OF HER CELL phone woke her and it took a full four rings before Domino oriented herself to the room. The laptop radiated heat and as she yawned, she made sure she'd logged out of the secure network before falling asleep (she had). Then she dug into the blankets to retrieve the phone.

"Weren't you just here?" she snapped, wondering what new information Darwin could possibly have for her so early in the morning.

"We've been together for two days and already you're tired of me."

Not Darwin. Luke. She cursed silently. The ring had been different and she'd been too exhausted and too distracted to notice.

She was getting sloppy. She had to regain control or she was going to blow everything.

"Sorry," she said, relegating her voice to a sensual purr. "I was dreaming about you."

"Can't imagine a dream would be better than reality," he replied, his voice husky.

She shifted in the bed, tossing a pillow behind her neck. Warmth flooded through her at his words and for the moment, she allowed the satisfaction to pool in her belly and below. "There's a difference between dreams and reality?" she asked.

"Not with us."

He had no idea.

"Where are you?"

If nothing else, she needed a chance to do a little more snooping around today. Last night's forage into The Shadow computer system had resulted in a lead she wanted to follow regarding Luke's half brother. She dug a little deeper and discovered that Marcus D'Angelino—he hadn't used the name Brasco since he turned eighteen—had been in prison for five years already on a fifteen-year term for embezzlement that he'd received at age twenty-two. Seemed a rather stiff penalty for a first time offender, so she'd decided she needed more inside info. Unfortunately sex with Luke had worn her out. Her planned catnap had morphed into a solid six hours of erotic, dream-filled sleep.

"I have a meeting with my accountant," Luke replied.

"How long will you be?"

"Don't you have work to do today?"

She chuckled wickedly. "I'm flexible."

"That I learned last night," he replied.

The man was insatiable. She liked that. "I can meet you this afternoon."

Luke was quiet for a moment before speaking. "Remember when we first met, I said I'd give you a tour of the city? I haven't made good on that promise yet."

Domino considered his offer. If he was just now starting his meeting, she'd have plenty of time to execute a quick recognizance and even review the computer files she'd downloaded last night. What more could she do without Luke's cooperation? As selfish and indulgent as a day exploring Chicago sounded, she decided what the hell. She'd turn the excursion into work somehow.

"Where do you want to meet?"

They set the time and place—a bar she could reach by taking the red line train to the Addison stop—then she disconnected the call.

During her shower, she tried to tamp down the anticipation she felt about enjoying an afternoon with Luke. Justifying that the "date" was simply another opportunity for her to delve even deeper into his world, she toweled off, dried her hair and applied a layer of makeup with exquisite care. Once she was dressed, she popped a bag of popcorn into her microwave for breakfast, pulled out a souped-up protein fruit drink as a chaser and reconnected to The Shadow network.

Per her request, she now possessed the full transcript of the trial against Luke's brother. What she read made the popcorn stick in her throat.

Yeah, he'd been arrested, tried and convicted for embezzlement. But the nature of the crime sat in her stomach like a two-ton hunk of iron.

Hacking.

Luke's brother, Marcus, had executed his crimes by breaking into the sophisticated computer system of a company he'd worked for as a technical consultant and then transferring the money into offshore accounts, covering his actions with the creation of phantom vendors and employees. He'd only been caught when he got greedy and deposited the ill-gotten gains into a bank in the city where an eagle-eyed teller noticed a discrepancy. As she read the testimony regarding Marcus's ability to navigate the complicated world of computer security, a thought popped into her head.

From the closet, she retrieved the papers she'd taken from Luke's safe, the ones she planned to return later this morning. What if Luke hadn't received this information from a Pentagon source? What if his brother had hacked into the system and the printouts were a result of his invasion?

What if Marcus had taught his older brother his tricks, thus explaining how the names of the embedded agents had been stolen without any clear source at the Pentagon.

Luke appeared to be on the most basic level with computers and all things technical, but she'd suspected earlier his lack of knowledge might be a ruse. Perhaps, she'd been right.

She considered calling Darwin, but decided she had a few other tasks to complete first. One of which now included meeting Luke for a day on the town—one that could end up his last.

AT LUKE'S REQUEST, Domino whipped off her blouse. Apparently the lacy black tank top worn over sleek black jeans and chunky boots wasn't appropriate for Wrigley Field. Through a crack in the shower curtain used to separate the tiny closet-size dressing room from the rest of the souvenir shop, Luke handed her a pale pink T-shirt.

She shoved it back out. "I don't wear pink."

Luke poked his head inside. "You need to broaden your color pallet."

She arched a brow. "Why am I suddenly worried about your sexual orientation?"

Luke's expression was incredulous. "After last night? You're a tough crowd. Look, the salesgirl just handed me that color pallet line when they didn't have your size in the black. I have no idea what it means."

Domino snatched the pink monstrosity and looked at it again. Okay, it wasn't entirely pink. The short sleeves were grey, matching a form-fitting stripe that would smooth down her sides. The Cubs logo front and center was a little much, but she'd come to Chicago to fulfill the man's fantasies, not her own.

"You like this?" she asked, holding the shirt out like a wet puppy.

"I haven't seen it on yet," he said, his tone saucy.

She took a miniscule step backward, since there wasn't much room, and stretched into the T-shirt with as much sexy undulation as she could manage in the enclosed space. The shirt barely reached her navel and hugged her breasts in ways that were all sorts of perfect.

"Maybe the pink isn't so bad," she mused.

Luke's dilated pupils added credence to her opinion. "Want to try the matching shorts?"

She pressed her palm on his forehead and pushed him out, slinging the shower curtain closed behind him. She supposed a pair of short shorts might not be the worst torture she'd ever endured, but being a fantasy woman didn't mean indulging each and every request. Men didn't like doormats.

And this man also clearly didn't like computers. She'd returned to his apartment this morning, tucked back the pilfered papers and completed one more thorough search of his place. If he was hacking into the advanced systems operated by The Shadow and the agencies it fed, he wasn't doing it from home—he had no computer there. And he wasn't doing it from his office, either. The system he kept there hadn't been updated in years and barely had enough processing power to run e-mail.

For the first time, she hoped he wasn't involved at all. That emotion—that deep need to clear him of any entanglement in this heinous crime—bothered her most of all.

She shoved the lace tank into her purse and emerged, doing a quick spin in front of the mirror. Actually she didn't look half-bad in the casual outfit and the pink did do an interesting thing to her face, bringing out natural skin tones that seemed to soften the effect of her blue-black hair. When he handed her a Chicago Cubs scrunchie for her hair, she nearly balked, but intrigued, she pulled her straight locks up into a ponytail and examined the final look.

"Not bad," she muttered.

Luke leaned in close from behind her, his hard body flush against hers. "Not bad? I'd like very much to sneak back into that dressing room and show you how hot you look."

The idea was tempting. "I know how hot I look, thanks."

With a wink, she headed toward a rack of long-sleeved hoodies and let him pay the bill.

Once the collection of Cubs paraphernalia (including matching seat cushions, a hat for him and a visor for her) was complete, they merged into the crowd making their way across Addison toward Clark to the entrance of Chicago's most famous baseball field. Domino tried, with relative success, to blend into the mass tangle of sports fans without allowing her instincts to overtake her. But once again, her mind slipped back to her initial training sessions with The Shadow, when bodies closing in on her from all sides meant danger.

She tensed. Her eyes darted to the sea of faces closing in on her from all sides.

Then Luke squeezed her hand, leaned in and shouted in her ear. "My wine vendor got us seats on the third base line."

She didn't know what he meant exactly, but the apprehension coursing through her bloodstream dissipated, even if she did realize that she'd begun to quiver, just as she had after making love with Luke in his office. Like an addict experiencing DTs, her body couldn't handle normalcy. For her, walking into a huge stadium not to pick off an attending nasty politician from a third-world dictatorship but to enjoy the actual game was as foreign to her as breathing underwater without scuba gear.

Passing through security progressed without a hitch, despite Domino's aversion to letting some rent-a-cop pat her down for weapons and dig into her purse. Of course, they could find nothing since she'd come relatively weaponless—another sensation she wasn't accustomed to.

She removed her cell phone from her purse and clipped it to the low-slung waistband of her jeans, glad she could at least stun someone with the apparatus inside the device. If she had to. Which she more than likely wouldn't.

And that was the oddest feeling of all.

"You look a little pale," Luke said, his eyes dark with concern.

She brightened her eyes and forced a smile. "I'm just craving one of those famous Chicago hot dogs you keep going on about."

A smile lit his face. God, he really was gorgeous, more so when he thought he was initiating something she'd enjoy, even something as simple as eating boiled pig intestines on a bun. "The best ones are not available everywhere in the stadium. You have to go looking."

She flicked the bill of his new baseball cap. "Then let's start our safari because I'm starved."

He hadn't lied. The combination of mustard, chopped onions, Serrano peppers, sweet relish, fresh tomato, a sliver of dill pickle and a dusting of celery salt on a hot dog nestled in a poppy seed bun was a burst of flavor she hadn't expected. She'd happily accepted his challenge to try mustard in place of ketchup. They laughed together as the mass of condiments spilled over the edges of their paper napkins and oozed onto their fingers. Domino was completely aware of people staring as they stood in the open-air food court on the upper deck licking the leftovers from each other's hands, and she didn't care. Mixing the taste of Luke's skin with the gastronomic delight of a perfectly steamed wiener was too delicious to pass up in lieu of more napkins.

"Did I lie?" he asked, taking a sip of the beer he'd balanced on a high table lined up around the vendors.

She licked up the last of the spilled relish from between her fingers. "You are clearly no liar when it comes to food."

"Want another?"

She laughed. "Want me to fit in these pants?"

"Not particularly," he responded, his eyebrows doing push-ups over eyes blue with freshly renewed lust.

She bit her bottom lip. Domino wasn't unaccustomed to men wanting her. She wasn't unaccustomed to men wanting her all the time. What was odd was that the same man wanted her, even after they'd had sex. Hot sex. It wasn't that men stopped wanting her after sharing her bed, but that she didn't stick around. And though she'd spent only two days with Luke Brasco, the experience somehow felt more prolonged. More significant.

Her cell phone vibrated against her hip. She checked the code on the display screen.

Darwin.

Urgent.

"I gotta take this," she said.

Luke nodded, a twinge of disappointment skittering across his face. "I'll grab us some peanuts and then we can head to our seats."

She flipped open the phone and stalked to the edge of the food court, where few people milled around to overhear.

"Why didn't you tell me hot dogs were so delicious?" she said, knowing Darwin was on the other end of the line.

"They'll kill you," her handler responded.

"That and about a million other things, especially in our line of work. What's up?"

"The buyer. He's on the move."

Domino straightened. A quick glance over her shoulder found Luke buying a huge bag of shelled peanuts from a vendor wearing a red, white and blue balloon hat twisted around his head. For a moment, the bizarre was completely normal. For a moment, Domino had forgotten why she was really here.

"Is he in Chicago?"

"Will be by tonight."

Darwin gave her the flight information and informed her he had a team in place to ensure that the alleged buyer was under constant surveillance.

"Anything new on the source?" Darwin asked.

Domino smiled and waved at Luke, who waited for her by the door that would lead them downstairs. He was looking in her direction, but didn't seem, suddenly, to notice that she was there. He was a million miles away.

Strange.

She snapped herself back to the conversation with Darwin. "I went through all the files on his computer and downloaded them to the techs for further examination. If they haven't found anything, neither have I."

"They've found nothing. But I do have one thing of interest to report on Gloria Brasco."

"That she's certifiably insane and Luke can legally have her committed to a locked-down facility?" she asked, hopeful.

Darwin's voice revealed no shared humor. "No, but she did visit a locked-down facility this morning."

"Where?"

"Statesville."

The prison. She'd gone to visit her son. Why?

"Tell me you had the visitor's room wired," she said.

"It's always wired. Unfortunately they were speaking in code."

"Code?"

Ice flooded Domino's veins. Was this it? The proof The Shadow needed to order her to eliminate Luke Brasco and now his family, too?

"Innocuous stuff, but clearly, the two of them know what they're talking about."

"And we don't?"

"Not yet," Darwin answered.

From the speakers placed throughout the stadium, loud, live organ music reverberated through the stands. Judging by the anxious look on Luke's face, the game was about to start.

"Orders?" she asked, waving again to Luke, indicating she'd join him in just a few seconds.

"Stick with Brasco. We still don't know if this is anything of significance. But our increasingly reliable source pegs Luke Brasco as the seller. Now that we know he has a brother adept at hacking computers and a mother who could be acting as a go-between, things aren't looking good for your boy."

Domino nearly claimed that Luke Brasco wasn't her boy. That she wasn't rooting for him one way or another. That she simply didn't care if her orders to eliminate him came through right here and now.

But instead, she clicked the phone shut. Lying to Darwin was a skill she'd simply never mastered and she didn't have the heart or the stomach to try to deceive him now.

9

AS THE TRAIN RUMBLED back toward the city proper, Luke shifted carefully on the hard plastic underneath him, trying not to wake Domino as she slumbered against his arm. At his insistence, they'd stayed for the entire game, then had beer and pretzels at the Goose Island Brewery. He wanted Domino to have the full Cub's game experience, from watching the Bleacher Bums in right field to singing "Take Me Out to the Ball Game," in homage to Harry Caray, at the seventh-inning stretch. For the first time since they'd met, Luke had, he thought, finally caught a glimpse of the real woman beneath the fantasy. One who probably wasn't accustomed to something so pedestrian as attending a ball game, but embraced the experience anyway. One who felt comfortable napping on his arm as the world streaked by outside the L. One who might, with some coaxing from him, end up the best thing that had happened to him in a long, long time.

Against his skin, she sighed and shifted, turning so that her forehead pressed against his shoulder and her face disappeared underneath a curtain of hair, loose now that the hair tie he'd purchased gave up trying to wrangle such straight, glossy strands. With his fingers, he toyed with the fringe, marveling at how a woman who fulfilled every physical need he possessed was now starting to meet deeper needs he hadn't, until now, acknowledged he had.

For the first time in years, he didn't feel destined to blow it in the love life department. The so-called Brasco family curse might not have been entirely vanquished, but he'd beaten back the bad mojo when it came to connecting with a woman and enjoying her company beyond just the sex. Only once—with Cecily—had he honestly tried to fight the cycle of failed relationships that had cursed the Brasco men for centuries. Since then, the idea of trying to establish any semblance of a committed relationship hadn't seemed worth the trouble. But now, with Domino, he couldn't help but think that maybe he'd found another chance.

Though he couldn't imagine a sensual, cosmopolitan creature like Domino standing in a garden, wrapped in a floral apron and wielding pruning shears as she trimmed rosebushes growing alongside her white picket fence, he could imagine waking up with her every single morning and going to bed with her in his arms every night. Just forty-eight hours ago, she'd been nothing but a sexual fantasy, the star of the ultimate wet dream. Now, she was warm flesh and hot blood and sharp tongue and brilliant mind and wicked sense of humor. She was more than he'd ever expected, and God help him, he didn't know what to do.

Today had been too much. He'd had no business going to the Cubs game once his accountant had broken the news about the books. The five thousand dollars he couldn't find amid this month's receipts had only been a drop in a bucket of betrayal. Three hours of poring through the ledgers revealed over two hundred thousand missing from various accounts—a transposed number here, an undocumented invoice there. Someone was bleeding him dry—and he had a very short list of who that someone could be.

When the train pulled into the station at Grand Avenue, Domino stirred. "This our stop?"

He could add amazing sense of timing and direction to her list of talents. He'd gone through with his plan to take Domino to the game because returning to the club meant confronting the one woman he'd trusted, even if she'd done nothing more trustworthy than marry his father.

"Yeah."

"What time is it?" she asked with a yawn as the doors mawed open and they followed the crowds onto the platform and then up the stairs to the street.

"Near seven."

"Wow," she muttered, her voice still raspy from yelling at the umpire after a particularly bad ninth inning call. "You've got to get to the club, huh?"

He glanced around. They were barely a block from the club, but if they overshot, they'd be strolling up the Magnificent Mile just in time for sunset over the city. He wished they were at the lake, maybe on Navy Pier. Or at least, Grant Park, where the deepening of the sky from bright azure to deepest midnight-blue would happen just beyond the impressive fountain. Still, he loved the rapid pace and frenetic quality of the city. He didn't need parks or bucolic settings to find romance in Chicago. The city brimmed with it. Hell, he could find romance wherever he was, so long as Domino still had her hand cupped in his.

"Luke?"

He stopped walking. God, his mind was going in so many directions, he couldn't even hold a conversation with the one person he wanted to talk to most of all.

"Sorry."

"You're in another world," she commented, her tone neither chastising nor overly concerned. Just matter-of-fact.

"I've got a lot on my mind."

"Worried about not being there when the doors open?"

He had to take a moment to process what she meant.

"You mean the club?"

"No, I meant the seventy-five-percent-off sale at Marshall Field's. Yes, the club."

"To be honest, the club is the last place I want to be."

"Excuse me?"

He chuckled humorlessly. He never thought he'd say that out loud. He never imagined he'd think it. But the fact remained that his beloved club was now a crime scene. Someone had been siphoning money from him for months. Someone he trusted. More than he should, he wanted to share his dilemma with Domino, but he held back. She wasn't his girlfriend. They hardly knew each other. He had to be realistic—they were lovers who knew next to nothing about each other's lives, pasts and future plans.

But he wanted that to change. God help him, he did. Was now the time? Was this the right situation to lead her deeper into his life?

"Never mind," he said, flipping what was left of her ponytail. He had to do a little more digging into his own life and finances before involving her. Their boundaries had been drawn the first moment she'd slinked into his club and ignited fires of lust and desire he hadn't felt in a long time. If he tried to break through the lines too soon, he might lose her for good. Women like her tended to retreat from such maneuvers and the last thing he wanted was to drive her away before he'd given their affair a fighting chance.

"Tonight won't be that busy," he pointed out, "but we can go around through the back entrance if you want."

"Trying to hide me?" she asked, eyebrow arched.

"No, I'd just rather not go inside looking like a Bleacher Bum. Tends to take some of the glamour out of the club's reputation."

She smoothed her hand through her hair and when the realization of what a mess her mop had become thanks to the elements registered on her face, he couldn't help but laugh.

She scowled. "I'm not used to being messy, okay?"

He snagged her by the waist and pulled her close, ignoring all the pedestrians who had to walk around them to continue on their way. With her scent snaking into his nostrils, with her warmth curling against his skin, he could oh-so-easily ignore the troubles weighing heavier and heavier on his mind. She smelled like hot dogs and popcorn and beer and fresh air and mowed grass and woman. He wanted to take a taste of her right here and now. Forget that someone was stealing from him. Forget that this betrayal could very well be one he could never, ever forgive.

"You look good enough to eat," he said.

She laughed and patted her stomach. "Don't mention food! You stuffed me with so much ball field junk, I'm going to be moving like a slug tomorrow."

"I can think of quite a few physical activities where a snail's pace works just fine."

She playfully pushed him away, grabbed his hand and trudged forward toward the club. "You have a one-track mind, don't you?"

He wished. More than anything, he wanted to shut down and concentrate on nothing but Domino. He wanted to feel her body beneath his, on top of his, beside his. He wanted sexual ecstasy to override thoughts of stolen money and lies and betrayal. He'd enjoyed every moment today with Domino, out in the open air, wrapped up in the simple act of watching a ball game with a woman who'd clearly never seen the sport live before, but he couldn't chase away his responsibilities any longer. Not when the survival of his club depended on finding out who would steal from him— and why. His continued success wasn't the only thing at stake. He had employees to think about. Creditors. Developers waiting for the least chink in his financial armor so they could take the building left to him by his father.

And therein lay the biggest trouble of all. In all his

efforts to keep from succumbing to the criminal instincts bred into his blood by his ne'er-do-well ancestors, he'd become a victim. Of his own stepmother.

"Do you have any family?" he asked.

They started walking toward the club again. He expected Domino to bristle or hesitate at his question—she seemed the type to embrace privacy. But she answered with candor that both surprised and intrigued him.

"No, actually. My father died when I was very young and my mother sort of lost it. She was in an institution for years. She's dead now, too."

He stopped. That was one hell of an admission from a woman whom he thought for sure would claim all personal information off-limits.

"Wow. I'm sorry," Luke said. "My mother died when I was a kid, too."

She crossed her arms over her chest and rocked back on her heels. Despite how candid she'd been, the topic made her uneasy. Something else they shared.

"How old were you?" she asked.

"Six," he replied.

"So you went to live with your dad?"

"And Gloria," he said, nearly choking on the name. God help him, but after his conversation with his accountant today, he couldn't help but suspect his stepmother first. She had access. She had his trust. Why she would betray that trust was an unanswered question. She'd kept him around after his father's disappearance, even though they had no blood ties. She'd raised him as best she could, coming up short in the nurturing department, but providing him with basic care. She'd fronted him the money for his business ventures long before he'd gained access to the trust his father had surprisingly had the forethought to leave for him. Sure, he knew she'd sold off some of the real estate that had become hers after his father had been declared dead in order to pay his half brother's legal fees, but otherwise, he'd had no reason to think Gloria was hurting for money. He couldn't even remember the last time she'd asked for a raise. But then, why ask when you can take?

Embezzlement. It clearly ran in the family.

"When did your dad die?" she asked, twining her fingers with his.

Luke lifted their clasped hands. Such a simple gesture, but perhaps, even more intimate than what they'd shared in the bedroom. Especially when paired with the conversation. He knew next to nothing about her, and yet opening up about his sordid family history seemed right. Natural. "I was ten when he disappeared."

"Disappeared?"

With a swing, he dropped their connection and shoved his hands in his pockets. The whole thing seemed so surreal to him now, so many years after the sting of abandonment had worn off. But then? He'd been so angry. So sad. So confused by how one parent could up and die before she'd hit thirty-five and the other could disappear into the night without a trace.

"One night, he just never came home. Dad was mixed up in all sorts of shady deals, but Gloria held out hope that he'd turn up someday. Then eight years later, after all the private investigators came up empty, after the money started to run out and we needed the influx from his insurance to keep his buildings going, Gloria had him declared dead. His own father had been murdered by the mob when he was a kid, leaving him with next to nothing, so he'd set up a trust for me, though I couldn't access it until I was twenty-five. Gloria made sure I had what I needed, though. Never wrote me off, even though I wasn't her kid."

"How generous of her," Domino said, her tone only slightly sardonic.

Yeah, well, he'd thought so, too. Until this morning. But he couldn't jump to conclusions. Just because she was the only person with easy access to his books and accounts didn't mean she was guilty.

Right?

"So your dad was in real estate?" she asked.

Sounded so classy when put that way. "He was more like a slum lord, truth be told. His family has been in Chicago for a long time. He inherited what little he had from his mother's family and managed the best he could. Some properties, like this one," he said as they approached Club Cicero, "were pretty damned valuable by the time he lit out."

"Why do you think your dad disappeared?"

Luke stopped and stared. Wow. He knew Domino had chutzpah, but few people ever asked the question straight out. Oh, they all wanted to know. Even Luke wanted to know. But few people ever had the guts to ask.

"I think fatherhood didn't agree with him. He left

my mother as soon as I hit the terrible twos. He left Gloria when Marcus was about the same age."

Domino winced. "Nice guy. Hope you didn't inherit his gene for parental responsibility."

Luke laughed loud enough for the people walking beside them to stare oddly. "I'm not taking any chances. No kids for me. What about you? Are there rug rats in your future?"

Over the years, Luke had learned that women generally responded to this question in one of two ways. They either launched into long, detailed diatribes of maternal enthusiasm, culminating in the sharing of the chosen names for each of their as-of-yet unborn sons and daughters, or they reacted as if someone had just told them their armpits stunk.

He would have guessed Domino to be a candidate for group number two, but she merely looked at him as if he'd just spoken to her in a foreign language.

"I've never thought about it."

He believed her.

They reached the back entrance to the club and as much as Luke would have rather explored this topic with Domino, he had something more pressing to do. He unlocked the back door and gestured her inside. She went immediately to the doors leading to the rooms upstairs and turned, disappointed, when he didn't follow.

"I've got a few things to do down here. You'll come down later?"

She tortured him with a pout. "Maybe I will, maybe I won't."

"God, tell me you're teasing."

She rewarded his desperation with a smile, then disappeared.

He turned toward the club and despite his grubby appearance, decided the dirty work had to be done. Now.

DOMINO WENT IMMEDIATELY to her room. Hearing what sounded like a ruckus in Gloria's room, she eased down the short hallway and gave a listen at the door. Sounded like Gloria couldn't find her favorite black pointed hat or something, because she was clearly tossing her belongings around and cursing up a storm.

Uninterested in the woman's histrionics, Domino went to her own room and peeled out of the clothes she'd worn to the game, lingering with her hands on the hem of the T-shirt Luke had bought her. This was, perhaps, the first gift she'd ever received. From anyone. Ever. She imagined she might have celebrated Christmas or her birthday in those years before her father died and her mother went bonkers, but the past seemed so cloudy, so unreal. Since her recruitment by The Shadow, she rarely thought of such things. They'd created a new world for her. One filled with espionage and hidden agendas and killers and political consequences of the most dire sort. Dealing with international terrorists and corrupt corporate gladiators bent on the destruction of the last super power, she hadn't had time to watch baseball or shop for trinkets or even share a pretzel and a beer with someone she didn't have to…

She sank onto the bed, stunned.

Someone she didn't have to kill? That determination had not yet been made. Sure, the evidence hadn't exactly panned out against Luke, but he was nowhere near free and clear. He'd gone to see his accountant this morning and ever since, despite his best efforts to show her a good time and concentrate completely and totally on her, she'd known he'd been distracted. The news he'd heard from his financial advisor had obviously not been good and needing money was a powerful reason for someone to betray his country.

She showered, changed into club clothes—a minis-cule swath of a skirt covered in dark green sequins, a triangle top, spiked bronze heels, matching jewelry and long, neck-sweeping earrings—and then dialed in to speak to Darwin. As she waited for him to answer, she glanced in the mirror. The outfit brought out her Asian-like features. Almond-shaped eyes. Silklike skin. Small hands and feet. She'd always loved the way she looked, but she'd never once questioned how her exact transfiguration had come to be. Had her father had Asian blood or her mother? Did her olive-skin come from Italian or Greek ancestry? She had a pro-pensity for ultrahot food. Was she Mexican? Indian? Did it matter?

Darwin finally answered. "Sorry for the delay."

"Is the target moving?"

"Negative."

Domino felt her stomach drop. What if the source had been totally unreliable from the start? She could be pulled from the mission in a heartbeat—and then what? What if she never saw Luke again? Why did that matter? God, she'd let him under her skin. He mattered to her. Damn it all to hell, but he mattered.

"Is this good or bad?" she asked.

"Buys us more time to find the information before it's sold. Our target has just picked up a very large amount of cash in a prearranged drop."

"So it could be tonight."

"Or not," Darwin pointed out.

"What about Brasco? Did you bug his accountant's office?"

Darwin filled her in on all they'd learned through wiretaps and various other listening devices. The news should have cheered her—clearly, the financial troubles plaguing Luke Brasco had not been going on for a long time—at least, not to his knowledge. Until today, he'd had no idea someone was sucking the lifeblood out of his business and personal accounts. He had no pressing reason to be arranging the sale of government secrets. Sure, he'd received large influxes of cash at various times over the last few years, but all were securely tied to real estate transactions or bank loans. Nothing fishy at all.

"So Brasco's in the clear?" she asked, hating how much she wanted the answer to be affirmative. The fact of the matter was, she no longer had any interest in eliminating Luke Brasco, guilty or not. If he ended up the source, she'd have had to grapple with emotions and moral choices and brain-splitting dilemmas she thought now were best left alone.

"He could be stashing the money in an offshore account that we haven't found."

"And just leaving it there without touching it?"

"People commit treason for reasons other than greed," Darwin concluded.

Of course they did. But even if she hadn't known Luke Brasco that long, she couldn't imagine that any of those myriad rationales applied to him.

"Next move?" she asked.

"Keep your eye on Brasco and continue checking out those working around him."

His stepmother topped the list, judging by the report from the accountant. Only one person could have stolen like that from Luke—Gloria.

"And?"

"Keep in contact with us at all times. If we cannot locate the source, we will take out the courier. That will be your job. I'm transmitting the latest Intel on our pigeon. You'll be our final defense. Hope you're still on your game."

Darwin emphasized the last word with a little more umph than she deemed necessary, as if he meant to chastise her for taking a few hours today to see the Cubs lose to the Cincinnati Reds. Well, screw that. She deserved a little fun, damn it. Something she hadn't really embraced until Luke Brasco slipped into her life.

"I can still hit it out of the park," she countered, confident she could still do her job with her usual efficiency—so long as Luke wasn't her target.

Darwin said no more, so Domino disconnected the call and decided that her best vantage point, after checking the monitors, was down in the club. She didn't see Gloria behind the bar and she also couldn't find

Luke among the throng that had gathered. Now that she knew why he'd been so distracted this afternoon, she could also anticipate his next move—a confrontation with his stepmother.

After locking up her equipment, Domino sealed her room, activated her security protocols and then started downstairs. The eerie silence in the hall caught her attention. Just what had Gloria been looking for earlier that had had her in such a snit?

Domino moved stealthily down the hall and listened at the door. She heard no movement, no voices. She rapped lightly and the door surrendered beneath her touch. Since she couldn't walk around Club Cicero with a gun strapped to her—she tended to spontaneously lose her clothing whenever she and Luke were alone for more than ten minutes—so she'd have to enter unarmed.

The unlocked door creaked as she pushed it open. She waited to see if anyone inside reacted to the sound, but no one did. Only slightly larger than her own setup down the hall, Gloria's room was a mess. Clothes, papers, books and videos littered the floor. The kitchen, though devoid of dirty dishes or rotting food, was a mass of plates, cups, silverware, recipe books and various and sundry paperwork. In the bedroom, a private area off to the side, the mattress was torn and askew. Gloria had been looking for something. But what important thing had she lost today, besides her stepson's trust?

On a hunch, Domino exited the room, leaving the door unlocked just as she'd found it. She crept up the stairs to

Luke's room and found his hallway door unlocked as well. Her skin prickled with an unfamiliar emotion—fear—but she shook it off and proceeded inside.

In Luke's room, she found Gloria. A combination of relief and satisfaction warmed her blood. Domino leaned softly against the door, which clicked closed beneath her weight, and then cleared her throat.

Gloria spun toward her, her eyes wide, her hair wild, her mouth slashed in a grimace. She didn't speak, but the hatred in her eyes communicated all that needed to be said.

Domino pulled herself up to full height, prepared for a fight.

"Now if this isn't the ultimate irony, I don't know what is."

_10_

LUKE STEPPED BACK inside his office and gestured Mikey inside. Something was wrong. Not only had he caught his bouncer sneaking beers during his rounds, but Gloria had disappeared. No one had seen her all day and his backup bartenders had had to do inventory and stock the bar for tonight without Gloria's direction. He'd asked Sienna to check her room upstairs, but she claimed no one answered her knock. Something had been odd in her expression when he'd followed up with his waitress—he made a mental note to investigate himself at the first opportunity.

But first, he had to see what was going on with his chief of security.

"You know I don't like my employees drinking on the job," Luke said.

Mikey had the decency to hang his head. "I know, boss. I started at home and couldn't get myself to stop."

"Something I can do?"

Mikey bit the inside of his mouth. "No."

"You need to take the rest of the night off." Luke dug into his pocket and extracted his key ring. "Crash upstairs. Take the bed and I don't want to see you again until tomorrow morning."

Mikey nodded and shoved his hands deeply into his pockets, his balance wavering.

Great. This was all Luke freaking needed. Now he'd have to cover for his most reliable employee when he should be searching for the woman who had likely stolen a truckload of money from him.

Mikey moved to leave, but Luke placed his hand on his bulky arm. "Look, man. We all got shit days, okay? You've never screwed up here before. Consider this one a freebie."

Instead of seeing relief, Luke watched Mikey's irises darken and his lips bare back into a snarl. He pulled the keys out and tossed them across the office. They slammed against a file cabinet and clattered to the floor. "I don't need your sympathy, okay?" he snapped. "I screwed up. Fire me. I don't give a shit."

Luke stood straighter. His head bouncer might be physically imposing to most, but to hell with it if Luke was going to be intimidated. "I don't want to fire you, but you can bet your ass I will if you push me. Clean up your act, Mikey. You're going to screw up your whole life if you don't figure out what you want."

Their gazes clashed. Mikey's lips twitched, as if he wanted more than anything in the world to tell Luke to go to hell, but he held back. Without another word, Mikey slammed out of the room.

Luke stared after him for a minute, stunned. He should go after him. He'd known Mikey for a long time and clearly, the guy needed someone to unload on. Luke cursed and retrieved his keys, realizing that in his preoccupation with his own life, he'd missed a chance to act like a human being rather than an uptight club owner with profit margins shoved up his ass. He was moving to the door when Sienna dashed inside, breathless. Could his day get any worse?

"What happened to Mikey?" she shouted.

Mikey had left the door open and the club tunes pounded behind them. Luke attempted to wave her off, but she charged inside and shut the door behind her. Fists on hips, she was ready for battle—a fight Luke simply didn't need.

"What did you do to Mikey? He had a really bad day today, okay? I think something happened with his wife."

Luke's heart dropped into his stomach. "The babies?"

Sienna sneered. "No, I think the embryos are fine. But I heard him talking to Craig and, I don't know, he and that twit he married had a fight or something. I didn't get a chance to talk to him—we've been so crazy busy with Gloria deciding not to show up. Maybe I should take my break now. Go after him."

Sienna had her lip in her teeth and Luke decided he had had enough of this girl going after his bouncer. It was none of his business, he knew, but Luke was fairly certain that whatever unhappiness had crept into Mikey's marriage, Sienna's constant overtures weren't helping.

"You'll have your break at your regular time. And if you chase Mikey down outside this building, you're out of a job, got that?"

Sienna stared at him, as shocked to hear his threat as he was that he'd made it.

"Who do you think you are, my father?"

Luke pressed his lips together tightly, trying hard to hold onto his professionalism. "No, I'm the guy who signs your paychecks. And the fact of the matter is, Sienna, you're causing problems for a valued employee that has been here longer and is harder to replace than you are. Keep that in mind. Now get back to work."

She spun away, yanking the door so that it slammed open against the wall. "You're just pissed because Gloria bailed tonight."

A move totally unlike his stepmother. She blossomed behind the bar. She loved the attention. She'd only missed a handful of nights since he opened the club. But she'd known he was going to see the accountant today. He figured she'd guessed what his financial expert would find.

"Sienna, you're sure she wasn't in her room?"

There was that look again. Uncertain. Guilty.

"Sienna?" he asked, insistence driving his tone.

"I didn't actually go up to her room, okay?" she admitted, her eyes rolling as if the little detail was entirely inconsequential. "I was trying to find Mikey and figure out what was wrong with him. But I called her from the break room and she didn't answer."

Luke groaned. He didn't have the time nor the energy to chastise his flaky waitress. He'd had enough with Mikey and had no idea how much energy he'd have to expend on Gloria once he caught up with her. He pushed past Sienna, ignoring her yelp of protest, and headed upstairs.

The state of Gloria's room caused his heart to drop

somewhere in the region of his toes. Was she looking for something she couldn't find—or did she tear the place up grabbing what she needed before she disappeared with his two hundred thousand dollars?

He found no answers amid Gloria's mess, so he stalked out of the room, pausing at Domino's door. He knocked. No answer.

Damn. He could really use Domino's help right about now. And that realization alone nearly knocked him to the ground. He didn't know what was more shocking— that he'd allowed himself to want Domino as more than just a lover or that the emotions she'd stirred up had overpowered his inbred, practiced cynicism.

Didn't matter. He'd deal with the consequences later. Right now, he had to find Gloria and at least establish that his stepmother hadn't done damage that couldn't be repaired.

Luke entered the stairwell and a female scream slid into his spinal cord. A second scream verified where he needed to go—his apartment. He pushed aside his surprise that the path was unhampered by locked doors, though shock slapped him hard in the face when he found Gloria pulling books from his living room shelves and heaving them at Domino's head across the room.

Domino easily deflected each blow. She seemed intent on simply holding her ground by the door, keeping Gloria contained.

"Holy hell, Gloria! What are you doing?" he shouted.

Domino punched a copy of *Jurassic Park* out of the air before it beaned Luke in the temple.

"Your stepmother objects to the fact that I asked her to stop trashing your apartment," Domino said, her tone clipped.

Gloria wailed, a sound that was pure violence and frustration. "She followed me up here! None of her business! None of this!"

Domino shrugged. "I don't know what she's talking about. Do you?"

Luke decided to ignore the fact that his lover and his stepmother were once again sparring. The location of their latest catfight also perplexed him, but he figured the details would sort themselves out eventually. He had more important fish to fry.

"Gloria, calm down."

"You asked her to spy on me, didn't you? Asked her to chase me down. Follow me, even," Gloria accused, her drama queen instincts in full force. "You wanted to embarrass me! Have the bitch you're fucking be the one to bear witness to my greatest humiliation."

True to her nature, Domino crossed her arms over her chest and stared blankly as the accusations started to fly instead of books. Unruffled and icy cool, she gave Luke a sideways glance, never taking her eyes off his stepmother in case she resumed her literary assault.

"Maybe I should leave," she offered.

Domino's presence was pushing Gloria to near hysteria. She had a paperback loaded in each hand, but she was hunched over, trying to pull air into lungs that refused to cooperate.

He nodded, but when Domino eased past him, he couldn't help but snag her softly by the wrist.

"Stay close."

Before she nodded her assent, her eyes flashed. With what? Surprise? He supposed the request was, like their handhold earlier today, a sign of something deeper between them. Something he couldn't yet name. Something that had no business being named this soon into their relationship.

Yet it was there, wasn't it? Trust. Need. Reliance. Luke couldn't deny the presence of the emotions coursing between them any more than he could refute that the next few minutes of conversation would be the hardest he'd ever exchanged with anyone.

Domino exited the apartment and closed the door, though it wasn't locked. He was comforted, knowing that Domino was likely on the other side. The last thing he wanted was to retell this story once all was said and done.

He turned back to his stepmother, his hands stretched out in surrender. "Okay, she's gone."

"You brought her here to investigate me, didn't you? I know the type. She's a spy—I'm sure of it! She's going to kill me if you give her a chance."

Luke took in a series of deep breaths. Gloria wasn't exactly young anymore, but he never considered the fact that she might be suffering from dementia.

"Gloria, Domino is a photographer," he insisted, though now that he thought about it, he'd yet to see her camera. Still, calling her a spy was loony. "I didn't send her to do anything."

For the first time since he'd entered, he took a look around. Just like her own room downstairs, the place had been turned upside down. Drawers turned out.

Shelves emptied. Rugs torn aside. But she hadn't gotten much farther than the living room. The kitchen seemed untouched. Domino had clearly interrupted before Gloria had had a chance to do much damage beyond the first room she'd entered.

He took a step forward, his hands still outstretched. "Glo, what were you looking for?"

"The papers," Gloria admitted, her eyes reflecting a look of abject defeat.

"What papers?"

"Don't play stupid with me, Luke. The papers you've been holding over Marcus all these years. Your brother needs to be free. Enough is enough. He has a chance to apply for parole this week and he'll get it, too, if no one objects. That means you. I can't have you showing up with evidence of further misdeeds. I want this over and done with, do you hear me? He's paid his dues!"

Luke took a step backward. He hadn't thought about those papers in years, since he'd used the evidence to make sure his brother learned his lesson. He'd locked them up safe and sound just as he'd promised after Marcus had pleaded guilty to embezzlement. His half brother had gone to prison for using the computers at his workplace to hack into secure systems and transfer money to offshore accounts, but before that crime had come to light, Marcus had used Luke's computer to work his way through the security at the Pentagon. When Luke had confronted him with the evidence found carelessly abandoned on his printer, Marcus had claimed he'd found nothing damaging to national security. Luke didn't know if he'd been lying or not—he hadn't wanted to know. He'd only wanted the madness to stop.

As a juvenile, Marcus had sported a rap sheet that rivaled *War and Peace* in length. All for computer crimes, each escalating in gravity and danger. Gloria had made excuses for her baby. Claimed he was just too smart for his own good—too bored with ordinary schools and jobs not to want more from life. As the older brother, Luke had finally shown some tough love. He'd used the Pentagon papers as blackmail, forcing Marcus to plead guilty and do his time. It was one thing to steal millions from a private corporation. It was something else entirely to break into secure government systems and download information, no matter how innocuous it all looked to his civilian eye.

"Marcus isn't the issue here, Gloria. I gave up spending time and energy on him years ago."

"And that's the problem, isn't it?" she snapped. "You wouldn't help us. You made him plead guilty!"

"He was guilty," he answered calmly.

"But he's serving a full term!"

"He shouldn't have stolen what wasn't his. He didn't steal bubblegum from the corner store, Gloria. He took nearly two million dollars from a company that eventually went bankrupt. How many people lost their jobs because of him? And what about the company owners? They put every last penny, not to mention blood, sweat and tears, into that venture just so an employee they trusted could take it all away?"

The similarities between that situation and his own

differed only in scope. Luke had thought he knew how the victims of Marcus's crime had felt before. Now, he was certain.

"Look, Gloria, Marcus doesn't want anything to do with me and frankly, that's probably best for all of us. He's old news."

"He's not! On top of his parole, he's filing an appeal. I need attorneys and I need you not to hold that Pentagon crap over his head."

Luke shook his head. He had used the information to force his half brother to plead guilty on the embezzlement charges and take the full sentence. He'd thought a long stay in a federal facility would do what countless slaps on the wrist had not—clean up his brother's act.

"I just wanted him to do his time and maybe, for once, learn a lesson."

"What lesson? That you can't count on family to protect you? That you can't depend on your own blood to help you out of a jam?"

"A jam? He stole two million dollars, Gloria. You've been making excuses for him for years. God," he said in frustration, punching the air with his fists. "Marcus does not explain why you stole money from me! Two hundred thousand dollars, Gloria. Two hundred thousand. Care to justify that?"

She stood straighter. Raised her chin. "I needed to pay the attorneys."

"So you stole from me?"

"You wouldn't give me the money."

"You didn't ask."

"You wouldn't give me the money for his attorney the first time. Why would you do it now? I'm a proud woman, damn it. I wasn't going to beg."

"But you'll steal?"

"You have plenty of money."

"I *had* plenty. Now, I'm back to scraping by. You sold off nearly every one of dad's real estate ventures before I came of age. Then you sold the last pieces you owned to pay for Marcus's bogus defense. This building and this club are all I have. Two hundred thousand isn't chump change, Gloria. You're going to pay me back. Every goddamned penny, you got that?"

Then his stepmother did something that Luke didn't expect. The tears weren't a surprise—no woman he knew was beyond turning on the waterworks if the display would work to her advantage. But Gloria went for broke. She wailed as she fell to her knees, the sound nothing less than the ripping apart of her arterial walls. Her face dissolved as tears streaked down her cheeks and her shoulders seemed determined to meld into her chest. Luke fisted his hands until his knuckles locked, but he couldn't witness this and remain unaffected. She wasn't just some employee with her hand caught in the cookie jar. This was a mother desperate to save one child and willing to exploit the other one to do it.

Making shushing noises, Luke dropped to the ground beside her and wrapped her in his arms. Great heaving sobs soaked into his sleeve as the full breadth of Gloria's sadness washed out in a tidal wave. He found himself stroking her hair, soothing her with guarantees he knew he shouldn't speak aloud, but that came from his heart and not his head.

Maybe Marcus had learned his lesson. Maybe he had been harsh when he'd pushed his half brother to plead guilty rather than fight the charges against him. And though he never in a million years would have used the evidence of the Pentagon break-in against his own flesh and blood, neither Marcus nor Gloria trusted their tenuous family ties with Luke. He'd given them no reason to.

When her wails subsided to manageable whimpers, Luke helped her onto the couch, poured her a shot of whiskey, then asked her to wait. He shuffled through his bedroom and with a deep breath, opened the tile in the bathroom floor. It took him a minute to remember the combination, but once he did, he unlocked the safe and extracted the evidence he'd kept all these years. He couldn't be his brother's keeper anymore. Not when his actions were tearing his stepmother apart.

He held the folded sheaths out to her, shaking them until the rattling sound broke through the last of Gloria's malaise.

"Here," he said. "Take them. Do what you have to for Marcus. With my blessing."

DOMINO FOUGHT THE URGE to launch herself through the door. Men! Couldn't he see how Gloria was playing him? She'd had a bad feeling about Gloria Brasco since the moment they'd met, but instead of following her carefully honed instincts, Domino had categorized the woman as a typical overbearing mother and had dismissed her as a suspect. Now, she knew differently. From the minute Gloria accused her of being a spy, Domino knew.

Took one to know one.

Gloria was the source. And Luke knew nothing about it.

Now, Domino simply had to prove it. And when she did? She'd have her order to kill. While part of her lightened at the realization that she would not have to take out the man she'd come to care for, the other part of her wasn't blind to the big picture. Luke loved his stepmother. She'd lied to him, stolen from him, manipulated him and yet there he was on the other side of the wall, offering her his one piece of leverage, giving her what she'd been willing to rip his home apart to find. How would he feel if he ever discovered that Domino had killed her in cold blood?

Wouldn't matter, would it? He'd never know. Domino would do the job and disappear. She'd be nothing more to him than a shadow of a lover who vanished into the night, never to be heard from or seen again. Even if she had to take Gloria Brasco out right in front of Luke's eyes, the consequences would be none of her concern. She'd move on. To the next mission. The next target. The next death.

Domino pressed her forehead against the wall and tried to push away the raging river of emotions coursing through her. For the first time in her entire career, she cared about the damage she left behind. She wouldn't mourn Gloria if indeed she was the source. The woman's selfish actions in the past had led to the deaths of Shadow agents who'd put their lives on the line to ensure the security of an entire nation. And the plan to sell the names of the agents deep undercover in Europe and the Middle East would not only jeopardize years of intelligence work, but could very well be the impetus for yet another, perhaps even more catastrophic, terrorist attack on American soil.

But protocols precluded her from explaining any of this to Luke. All he'd know was that the woman he'd taken into his bed had murdered his stepmother. How would he live with that knowledge?

How would she?

When Luke put his hand on her shoulder, she jumped and was halfway through a defensive maneuver when Luke's protests of, "It's me, it's me," broke through her embattled brain.

He released the arm she'd twisted around his back.

"Sorry," she murmured.

He rubbed his sore shoulder. "What is it about me tonight? Did someone stamp 'kill me' on my forehead or what?"

Not surprisingly, his attempt at a joke fell flat. She couldn't muster the acting ability to laugh, so simply stepped back and looked at her feet until she regained her composure.

"I wouldn't have killed you," she said, once she'd regained control over her crazed heartbeat. Only she knew how true that statement was. And only she knew the consequences of such an admission, even if the confession was made only to herself. So much had changed since she'd met Luke. Too much for her to process all at once, especially with him staring at her with the kind of exhaustion that came only from emotional upheaval like the one he'd just experienced.

On one hand, she couldn't understand how he could be so easily manipulated by the woman in the other room. But then, what did she know about families? The only cohesive unit she knew was The Shadow, and she trusted that they'd turn on her in an instant if she threatened the foundation of their operation in any way.

On the other hand, she envied that Luke cared so deeply about another human being that he was willing to give her the benefit of the doubt over and over again.

"Where'd you learn that shit, anyway? Military?"

"Not exactly," she replied. "I travel alone a lot. Girl has to be able to protect herself."

Suspicion flashed in his eyes. *Oh, sure. Believe every lying word out of your stepmother's mouth and then doubt me when I tell you I've had a little self-defense training?*

"I used to date a Navy SEAL," she admitted. It wasn't a lie, though "dating" was a euphemism for "fucked like bunnies" in between missions.

That explanation he bought, clearly, because he changed the subject.

"Did you hear?"

"Every word," she replied.

He ran his hand through his hair and she once again caught a glimpse of the complete emotional exhaustion the scene had wrought on him.

"I have a lot to explain," he said.

She shook her head. "Not to me. Not if you don't want to."

He reached out and ran a finger along her cheekbone, the contact soft and intimate, a figurative and literal reaching out that she couldn't deny. She leaned into his palm, closed her eyes and for a split second, allowed herself to revel in the sweetness of his touch. After the scene in the other room, she knew this couldn't last much longer. Gloria teetered on the verge of desperation and if Domino's instincts proved true, the situation would soon explode and Domino would have to act. Then, whatever she and Luke Brasco had started would cease. Instantly. Coldly. Cruelly.

But they had at least a few more hours. Perhaps a few more days. Despite the turn in her mission, Domino knew she had to take what she could from this relationship because chances were, she'd never have anything like this again. She no longer lusted after a promotion within The Shadow. She wanted to go back to the way things were. The isolation of her usual assignments saved her from the hurt now raging through her with the agony of live electrodes taped to wet skin. Leaving Luke would be the hardest task she'd ever been given and for a split second, she doubted she had the strength to comply.

"Let me calm Gloria down," he said. "Then I have to get back to the club and make sure the whole operation hasn't fallen apart. I sent Mikey home and Sienna's in a snit and with Gloria not on the floor—"

Domino silenced him with fingers pressed softly over his delicious lips. "Come to my room when you're done."

The words spilled out. She had so many secrets tucked away in her room, the invitation was risky. Still, she wanted him there. In her room, no one could watch them, hear them. For a few hours, they'd be truly alone.

He nodded, a tiny grin curving his lips.

"Want me to go down and check on the club?" she offered.

"Do you know what to check for?"

She shrugged. "Make sure no one is watering down the booze or that the bouncers aren't letting their friends in without paying the cover?"

He smiled, impressed. "There's a little more to it than that, but it's a start."

She leaned up, gave him a peck on the cheek and started down the stairs. She allowed herself a few more seconds of normalcy, until she slipped into her room and made quick work of stashing her equipment out of sight. Then, before heading to the club, she detoured to Gloria's apartment again.

One aspect of her story didn't add up. Sure, she could understand her trashing Luke's apartment in search of the evidence against her son. But what had she been looking for in her own place?

The list of agents' names, perhaps? And if she no longer had it…who did?

11

USING HER EARPIECE to monitor Luke and Gloria's conversation upstairs, which consisted of little more than Gloria reminiscing about when she and Luke and Marcus had not been at odds, sometime back in the eighties, Domino did a quick sweep of Gloria's room one more time. Closer inspection showed boot marks on the carpets that in no way could have come from any of the shoes in Gloria's closet, least of all the sequined sandals the woman had been wearing when Domino last saw her upstairs. Domino patched in to Darwin and asked him to review the surveillance footage from the club.

"Normal deliveries all morning." Pause. "Dairy. Bread. Liquor. Wait. Is that liquor again?"

He clearly wasn't asking her but the agent in charge of watching the comings and goings at the club.

Domino's chest froze. "Two liquor deliveries? Is that normal?"

"Hold on," Darwin said. "I have to synchronize some footage."

Domino held her breath, listening to the muttering from the other end of the line and wondering if someone associated with the buyer had gotten into the building right under their noses. The whole case could fall apart right here. A full five minutes elapsed before Darwin finally patched back in.

"We have unauthorized entry into the apartments about two hours ago."

Domino cursed. "Weren't your people monitoring?"

"We have our attention focused mostly on the buyer."

"What if he's a decoy?"

"We could file that under worst-case scenario. You need to determine for certain that Gloria had the list and that it is now missing. Can you do that?"

She contained a growl. "I can try. Gloria hates me. She isn't likely to open up to me."

"Work something out."

"I will," she insisted, though she had absolutely no idea how. For all of Gloria's histrionics earlier, Luke had calmed her down rather quickly. If she'd just lost the key piece of information that could earn her millions of dollars, would she be so calm now? Domino doubted it. Gloria might be a devious traitor, but she wasn't the grace-under-pressure type.

The clicking of keys and conversations on the other end of the line continued, even louder than before. The whole team had clearly been summoned.

"Anyone you recognize on the tapes?" she asked.

"Hard to tell. We need more time to review."

"Does it look like they got what they were looking for?"

More clicking. More waiting.

"The exit is hurried. Gloria comes in soon after. For all we know, these guys were just thieves looking for jewelry. And we haven't yet established that Gloria possessed the agent names to begin with."

Domino chewed her bottom lip. "Gloria has fairly close contact with her incarcerated son, right? And the guy clearly has the talent to infiltrate secure systems at the Pentagon. Is there any way he accessed that information years ago?"

"Explain."

Domino dropped down onto the bed, her mind racing as the pieces fell into place. "Most of the agents we're trying to protect have been imbedded for years. What if the names of those agents were stolen at the same time as the Pentagon manifests? Some of the intel would be out-of-date, but not the agents' names or the terrorist groups they're spying on."

"You think Gloria got the names of the agents through her son, and that the buyer tried to get them out of her apartment without paying."

"Yes, but I also think they came up empty or Gloria would be a raving maniac right now."

"Isn't she?"

Domino shook her head. "No, she was, but Luke has her calmed down. If she'd just lost information worth millions of dollars, she'd be inconsolable. She tore up her own apartment earlier, I heard her. Maybe the guys who broke in didn't mess up anything. She did it all herself."

"What was she looking for?"

"Her favorite nail polish? The mate to her favorite stilettos? Could have been anything. Maybe she's had the combination to Luke's safe for years, but just didn't know where it was located. If she realized the buyer was trying to make a move without paying, she might have been motivated to make sure that all evidence of Marcus D'Angelino's forays into the Pentagon systems were erased. Those agent names and locations are valuable. I find it hard to believe that she'd consider it safe to keep that information in hard copy in a place like this, where people come and go all the time. Either the list is at another location or she has it memorized."

Darwin didn't respond for a moment, then replied. "Your scenario is possible."

Domino listened as he ordered Marcus D'Angelino into immediate custody. She didn't know whether to sigh with relief that they'd nearly reached the end of this mission with Luke no longer pegged as a suspect or to worry that Luke could still be linked to the crime because he'd had the Pentagon papers in his possession. Without a doubt, she knew he'd had nothing to do with the selling out of his country. He cherished his honesty too much—he hated all things criminal.

Which was why she had to leave. To him, a killer was a killer was a killer, even if she was sanctioned by the government. He'd never accept who she was. She'd never ask him to.

Darwin's voice snapped her attention back to the phone. "Keep an eye on Gloria Brasco, though I'm sending another contingent of agents right now as backup. If the thieves did not retrieve the agent names from Gloria's apartment, then the buyer will try to contact her soon. If she does have the names memorized, you'll be ordered to eliminate her. Clean up this loose end. This case is coming to a head soon, Domino. You need to prepare yourself to leave."

Domino acknowledged Darwin's advice with a curt, "Affirmative."

"Domino," he said sternly, before she could disconnect the call.

She stared at the phone. She had her orders. What more could her handler want?

"I'm still here."

The pause was ripe, and Domino knew then that whatever Darwin wanted to say to her was of a personal nature. Didn't happen often—but it did happen.

"This exit may not be like the others," he warned.

Domino swallowed thickly. Darwin had been the one and only constant in her life since age fifteen. Though they'd worked hard to maintain a professional, detached rapport that kept them both alive, sometimes, Domino sensed that Darwin knew things about her that she didn't even know herself—particularly when it came to her feelings. In her line of work, emotions were messy, inconvenient and downright dangerous. Without another word exchanged, she understood Darwin's implied concern.

"I'm still on the job, Darwin. I'm always on the job."

With that, she flipped the phone shut and proceeded downstairs. Despite her assurances to her handler, she operated in a daze, her mind overloaded with the realization that soon she'd be gone and Luke Brasco would no longer be a part of her life. She checked on the club as she promised Luke and found everything running with surprising efficiency. Domino had to give Luke credit for hiring staff that could rise to the occasion of having their boss, their head bartender, their head of security and their most popular, if flaky, waitress all gone at the same time. But on a Sunday, the crowd was smaller, more subdued and completely satisfied with the two-for-one drinks.

She quickly toured the kitchen, impressed by the cook's able handling, then skimmed through the employee locker room for verification that no one was off taking a cigarette break when they were needed on the floor. The place was deserted. Or so she thought…at first.

She heard whispers in the back, behind the shower stall. Curious, she snuck over, not entirely surprised to hear Sienna's voice as she neared.

"Mikey, you think too much. Sometimes, you've just gotta let yourself go. You know, concentrate on what feels good here and now."

At the sound of Mikey's moans of pleasure, Domino expelled a frustrated breath, then turned and walked away. This was none of her business. She had her own issues to deal with and frankly, her situation with Luke made Mikey and Sienna look like Cinderella and her handsome prince. What happened or didn't happen between the waitress and the bouncer could destroy lives, but not in the way Domino soon would. With bullets.

And besides, in a lot of ways, Sienna had a point. Sometimes, concentrating on what felt good in the present beat the hell out of anticipating the loneliness of the future.

SHE KNEW MIKEY WAS DRUNK. She didn't care. Sienna had waited too long for this and she couldn't take her hands off of him even if she wanted to. Which she didn't. Once she ripped open his shirt and plied her palms to his chest, her skin adhered to his. God, his muscles were so big. So hard. She couldn't help but lean forward and take a smooth male nipple into her mouth and suck hard, making him hiss with pleasured pain.

She'd wanted him for so long. She could remember the first time she'd met him. Mikey Maldonado had literally filled the room with his extra large body and twinkle-eyed smile. From that first instant, her nipples had peaked hard underneath her blouse and her clit had quivered inside folds of moistening flesh. Lust was a powerful pull, one Sienna had never quite learned how to ignore.

When he tangled his hands in her hair, Sienna dropped lower, kissing a line down his abdomen, tugging with her teeth when she reached the path of hair stretching upward from his waistband. She deftly released the button and zipper until his jeans dropped and she could inhale the musky scent of him through the thin material of his boxers.

Before she could press her tongue against the fabric, he tugged her to stand. She'd lured him into a tiny corner behind the lockers, the only private place she could think of that was still in the club. Luke had threatened her job only if she left the club to seek out Mikey—he'd said nothing about cornering him inside. As much as she'd wanted to take Mikey home and make love with him all night long in her bed so that she'd be able to smell him in her sheets the next morning, she'd had to grab the chance while she had it. Yeah, he was intoxicated now, but once he realized how good they'd be together, he wouldn't need alcohol to give him the courage to take what he deserved.

"Sienna, I'm married," he slurred.

She reached into his shorts and took his impressive package into her hands. "Old news, baby. If you haven't noticed, I don't care about your marital status. I just know what I want and that's you."

He was hard and long in her palms. Even his balls had thickened in response to her deft handling. She stroked him the way she knew men liked. As if she couldn't get enough of him. As if she couldn't have him fast enough. He instantly responded. His head dropped back. He closed his eyes. He groaned, panting as she stroked and tugged and squeezed, all the time whispering how big he was, how she couldn't wait for him to drive inside her and show her what a real man felt like. What he felt like.

When she dropped to her knees, he gave up all protest. Power surged through her, the kind of rush that she experienced when a man surrendered completely. To her. To the undeniable want. To the natural sexual play they both needed so desperately.

He tasted like salt and sweat, but the flavors excited her. His skin was smooth and hot beneath her tongue. He quivered when she scraped her teeth across his flesh, increasing her need to take him deeper, do him right. He'd learn what a real woman could do for him.

Only she could make him feel this wanted, this strong, this manly. She knew this like she knew her own soul.

She coaxed him over the edge and drank him in completely. As he sat on the crate and recovered, she stripped down to her panties, removing her bra with slow, teasing precision. She pushed away the niggle of disappointment that he didn't seem to register the skill of her striptease.

She slapped him softly across his cheek, causing those big brown eyes of his to widen with recognition.

"You don't want to miss the rest of the show, do you, Mikey?"

Finally a grin. Sloppy and lopsided, but a grin anyway. He reached out and cupped her ample breasts, sending her soaring into the stratosphere with pleasure. She scooted forward so that he could have full access, which he took without reservation.

This was how it was supposed to be, Sienna realized, climbing across his lap so he could take her nipples between his teeth and tug with a little too much enthusiasm, truth be told, but she didn't care. All in all, the effect was the same. She was wet for him, hot for him and she could barely wait to have him completely.

Mikey seemed just as eager. He ripped off her panties and thrust his fingers deep inside her, jolting her with pleasure. She reached between her legs and found his sex, still slightly lax. She encircled him, tugged and rubbed until he grew hard enough to hold the condom she'd kept in her pocket just for this moment, never realizing that tonight would be the night she lived her greatest fantasy.

His eyes, glassy but intense, focused on hers as she climbed back on top of him. The minute he'd slipped fully inside her, he stood, grabbing her by the ass as he swung her around and pressed her hard against the wall. She locked her legs around his waist and hung on for the ride. Wild, hard, hot and sweaty, she absorbed every impact with pleasured cries. Yes! This was how she wanted it. Even through the redness coating his eyes, she stared into an intensity she'd always known existed, always wanted, always felt belonged to her. How could he ever forget sex this good? He wouldn't leave her. He wouldn't dismiss her. Not once they'd both tasted something so forbidden and yet, so right.

DOMINO OPENED HER DOOR to search for Luke, but didn't have to go far. He was standing in the hall outside her room, leaning wearily against the wall, looking like he needed a few weeks' worth of mindless sex followed by dreamless sleep to make up for the angst-filled scene he'd just experienced.

But she couldn't offer him more than tonight. The most she could provide was an hour or two of intense lovemaking. Enough to make him forget his stepmother's betrayal and for her to escape the inevitable knowledge that very soon, he'd no longer be a part of her life.

"Tough day, huh?" she asked.

"Started out badly," he replied wryly. "Got decidedly better—" his eyes twinkled with obvious memories of the ball game "—then it sunk to the bottom of the barrel."

She slipped her hands around his waist. "Where's Gloria now?"

"Sleeping. I can't believe I did this, but I just called Craig off the floor and asked him to wait outside the door. Something's up with her and I don't want her running off. No matter what reasons she may have had to steal from me, we've still got a lot to work through."

Domino smiled. He had no idea how his simple act of employing his own security staff to watch his stepmother had just freed her from the bonds of her responsibility to The Shadow. Okay, technically, she shouldn't allow Gloria out of her sight, but she couldn't have her in her sight so long as Gloria hated her, which she did. Darwin had sent agents to watch every entrance and exit and Luke had now arranged for security at the door. A few hours of personal time with Luke were an indulgence she couldn't resist, not when this could be her last chance to have the man who'd done something no other man ever had—he'd made her feel, for the first time in her life, like she could fall in love.

But love was only a possibility, if she wasn't who she was, and if she didn't have to do what she knew, soon, she'd have to do.

"Well, if she's shut up tight and the club is running just fine on its own—which it is, by the way—then why don't you come inside for a while?"

"I thought you'd never ask."

Domino opened the door and held her breath. She couldn't believe she'd done something so cheesy, but after witnessing the less-than-romantic pairing of Mikey and Sienna downstairs, she'd succumbed to inspiration. She'd raided the Club Cicero storeroom and after spiriting up several bags full of props, she'd set a scene borrowed from either a female-directed soft-porn flick or a man's idea of a classic romance film, depending on one's point of view. Luke chuckled as his eyes adjusted to the light, then turned, folded her into his arms and kissed her madly while kicking the door closed with a resounding slam.

"Like what I did with the place?" she asked, breathless.

He nuzzled his lips against her neck and toyed with the straps of her blouse. "Did you do something?"

She slapped him playfully and tugged away. "I'm not exactly the girlie type, if you haven't noticed. This was a big stretch for me."

He laughed, pulled her in front of him and surveyed the scene while grinding his increasing erection against her backside. "Well, honey, you stretch just fine."

The hunger in his voice reverberated against her skin as the heat from the candles suddenly made her clothes feel stifling. She must have lit two hundred votives in various colors and placed them on every flat surface she could find, including the floor. On the bedposts, she'd twirled a rainbow collection of feather boas. The crisp white sheets on the bed were now dotted with swatches of red and pink tissue paper, each scented like rose petals, a leftover, she guessed, from a private bridal shower or Valentine's Day event. For the first time in her life, Domino had thought only like a woman when she'd created the scene for her and Luke. She couldn't remember being a killer or an agent or anything but a woman who was now deeply, though temporarily, in love.

She twisted in his arms and undid the buttons of his shirt. "You don't think this is all too…predictable?"

"From you? This is the most unpredictable thing I can imagine."

She pouted prettily. "You think I'm not romantic?"

"No, *you* think you're not romantic. You see yourself as a modern, hard-edged woman grounded in realism. You make love because your body craves it and you keep your heart behind iron bars at all costs."

Domino stepped back, the teasing playfulness draining from her with those few truth-filled sentences. "Wow. You really see all that?"

He arched a brow. "Am I wrong?"

She frowned. "No, you're not wrong. I just didn't think I was so transparent." In her business, transparency was not a good thing.

But then, he'd tapped into the woman, not the agent. Remarkable.

"You're not transparent," Luke said, matching her undressing of him by tugging the straps of her filmy silk tank top down her arms. "You're damned hard to read."

She licked her lips, holding onto a sigh as his fingers dallied down her skin, igniting a flame that shot straight to her sex. She couldn't remember a man who could spark her so quickly, so easily and so innocently. How was she going to live without him?

She shook that black cloud of a thought away. Domino had lived in the moment for most of her life. Why stop now?

"Thanks for trying so hard, then," she replied.

"Do I get a prize for all my hard work?"

"Get undressed and I'll give you exactly what you deserve."

Luke did as he was asked in record time, without noticing at first that she hadn't done the same. He climbed onto the bed and found her staring at him, fully clothed and with a wicked gleam in her eyes.

"Will you be joining me this evening?" he asked.

She laughed at his maître d' imitation. "In a minute. I kind of like looking at you naked and nestled in all those feathers and rose petals."

"It's every man's fantasy," he quipped.

"Oh, and I thought this was."

She started to strip. Domino didn't need music or special lighting or any of the effects to make her removing her clothes the most erotic spectacle he'd ever watched. She took her time, her gaze locked with his as she revealed every inch of her flesh with painful, delicious slowness. The act was simple and honest and open and when she climbed over the sheets to join him on the bed, he thought he might burst for wanting her.

He immediately flipped her onto her back and proceeded to taste and discover every nuance of her skin. He slid his hands up her arms and locked them over her head, knocking the headboard. A feather floated down and landed on her shoulder, giving him an idea he couldn't resist exploring.

He plucked the feather off her skin and fluttered the breezy edge across her flesh.

"How does that feel?" he asked.

She smiled. "Tickles."

He flicked the feather lower, across the tips of her nipples. "A good tickle or a bad tickle?"

"What do you think?"

She shifted under his attentions, but he clucked his tongue. "You have to remain perfectly still," he chastised.

"Why?"

"Why not?"

The reply satisfied her and Luke spent the next delicious minutes brushing the feather across her body in a gentle exploration that required his total concentration. He noticed how her flesh erupted with tiny prickles as he swept the feather across the sides of her breasts and the inner softness of her legs. He inhaled the heady scent of her arousal as he drew the feather lower to tangle in the smooth strip of curls between her thighs. He couldn't resist easing her legs apart and with the same lightness as the feather, flicking his tongue into her and reveling in the soft coos of her approval.

He didn't rush. He didn't push. He tasted her softly, drawing her slowly into the vortex of need coursing through him. She slid her hands onto his shoulders, but didn't press for quicker action, which inspired him to slow down even further. He also took his time with her clit, sucking thoroughly until he knew she'd reached the boiling point.

And so had he.

He donned protection and slid inside her carefully, allowing his sex to feel every snug inch of hers. He pushed in deeply, then drew out, repeating the process until he'd melded with her beyond the physical. He watched her eyes, now wide with wonder, as they wordlessly made love the old-fashioned way. The way they never had before with each other. Or perhaps, with anyone else.

Luke closed his eyes tight and concentrated on the textures of her body beneath his. The soft skin of her thighs wrapped around his waist. Her breasts brushing against his chest. Her hard nipples inflaming his skin. He curved over her at the same time she arched her back, allowing him to suckle her softly as their rhythm increased. The tightness stretching through his body felt amazing, but with every stroke, with every taste, with every slip and slide of their wet and willing bodies, Luke's ability to think succumbed to his instinct to feel.

The orgasms were simultaneous, slow and long-lasting. He kissed her as they came, their tongues lazily sparring as he fought the instinct to push harder, pump faster. His reward was a languorous, long-lasting thrill coursing through him until the strength abandoned his arms and he eased on top of her, panting and satisfied. Over time, the warmth from the candles and the tickle of a few errant feathers against his nose made him open his eyes.

He rolled to the side, his gaze trapped by hers. Her face held a satisfied smile, but her eyes reflected a shine of confusion.

"What's wrong?"

"Nothing," she answered, swallowing hard. "Everything. It was so simple."

"Sex isn't complicated," he replied with a sardonic edge he didn't really intend.

She laughed lightly. "Usually, no. But with you, it is. You have no idea."

He leaned up on his elbow, loving how her lips were swollen from his kisses. "Why am I so complicated?"

"Because you've made me love you. And you weren't supposed to do that."

Luke opened his mouth to respond, but she blocked his reply with a finger across his lips.

"Don't say it back. God, that would only make things worse."

She wasn't kidding. And she wasn't wrong. Luke had never meant to care for Domino, especially in such a short time, but he couldn't deny that like a spy, she'd snuck into his consciousness and touched him in places he normally kept off-limits. He did love her. Crazy as it sounded after only a few days, Luke knew the emotions connecting them ran deeper than he'd ever experienced before and though he'd never admit it aloud, he was scared to death.

He kissed her finger, then broke her rule of silence. "The only thing that could make tonight worse is if you ask me to leave."

She shook her head emphatically. "Never. You may want to leave at some point, but I'll never ask you to."

They kissed again and Luke knew that was all the commitment he could handle for tonight. But tomorrow was another story altogether.

12

"YOU WERE RIGHT."

Domino forced her eyes open. She pressed the cell phone closer to her ear and replayed Darwin's confirmation in her mind. She wasn't exactly used to hearing those words out of Darwin's mouth, simply because it wasn't normally her job to be right or wrong. Ordinarily she simply followed orders. Then someone had gotten a wild hair up their ass to throw her into the unknown and see if she would sink or swim. Apparently she'd won the gold medal in the breaststroke…so how come she felt like the air was being squeezed from her lungs?

"Right about what?" she asked, still sleepy from her night of lovemaking.

"The information was stolen five years ago, at the same time as the Pentagon manifests. Luke Brasco caught his brother after his Pentagon system break-in, but only because he'd left evidence on the man's printer. Marcus D'Angelino had infiltrated several more secure systems around the same time and found a file containing the agents' identities and assignments, which he stole. Thanks to contacts he made in prison, he finally figured out how to use the information to his financial advantage."

"And his brother?" she asked, her throat tight as she pushed out the question. After what they'd shared in her bed last night, she couldn't imagine eliminating him for his part in any crime. She'd quit first. She'd disappear. "Any evidence of collusion on his part?"

"None," Darwin replied crisply. "Luke Brasco is now officially in the clear."

Domino sat up in the bed, absently running her hand over the cold spot Luke had vacated just after sunrise, and half listened while Darwin explained in detail how the hacking occurred in the first place and how Luke's computer whiz half brother had managed to cover his tracks. Computer science wasn't her forte, but she knew enough to understand that only a highly skilled pro could have broken through the walls that contained such classified information.

"This guy is good," Darwin assessed. "I have half a mind to push his parole through and then recruit him to our side."

"But you won't," she asserted.

"I don't think he'd last long once word gets out that he sold out U.S. patriots for cigarette money."

"Was that his motive?"

Domino had no illusions about traitors, but the money Marcus might have commanded for the rest of the high-level information clearly could have earned him enough to buy the whole of R.J. Reynolds and not just a couple of packs of Cools.

"Before he could get parole," Darwin answered, "Marcus had to pay restitution to the company he stole from. Apparently he'd tapped into those offshore accounts pretty deeply before he was caught. He had to make up the difference by selling a few of the names and clearing his debt."

"And he couldn't think of anything more enterprising than betraying his country?"

"We don't have all the details, yet. Our operatives are still…interviewing him. We believe he got the idea from an al Quaeda sympathizer he shared a cell with about two years ago. He was his initial contact."

"Have you been able to tie him to your informant?"

"Affirmative. We have no doubts this guy was the source."

Domino shook her head. Great. Just fucking great. Now, not only was Luke going to lose his stepmother, who'd clearly been the means Marcus used to pass the information along to enemies of the state, but his half brother, too. She doubted Marcus would be eliminated—he was now a valuable source of counterinformation. But Gloria? She knew government secrets. She had all the outside contacts. Unless she could prove herself valuable somehow to the government, she would be permanently stopped.

"So Gloria is the one the buyers will contact."

"Best guess, yes."

"Why'd she bother siphoning off two hundred thousand from Luke when she was looking at millions?"

Darwin clucked his tongue. "She didn't want to spend her cut on the attorneys needed for the parole, I guess. Marcus admitted that what was left of the restitution money went into his mother's pockets. I guess she didn't want to share."

Domino slid down into the pillows. God, if Luke only knew. He'd given this woman the benefit of the doubt. And now, because of her traitorous lies and actions, she was marked for death.

"What's your plan for Marcus?" she asked, knowing the pill of Gloria's elimination would be easier for Luke to swallow if he at least had his brother left behind.

"We're moving him to a maximum security prison under our control. He's managed to keep his skills finely honed on the computers in the prison infirmary. When the agents he compromised are all safely out of their assignments, he can bargain for his freedom, if we don't try him for high treason."

"Why not just take him out?"

"He retrieved the information, but barely had it in his possession before he went to prison for embezzlement. We don't believe he remembers any specifics of what he saw, but of course, we can't be sure. We're not about retribution on this one, Domino. Just about protecting our own. Gloria Brasco can't be tried through the courts. If the existence of our undercover operations becomes known, not only will our operatives around the world be in danger, but the crucial pipeline of information we've tapped into will be lost."

Domino took a deep breath and asked, "What are my orders?" even though she knew the answer.

"Marcus verified that his mother has the names of the agents. More than likely, she's not only committed them to hard copy, but she also has them memorized. She's your target. The order has been signed."

Domino's stomach dropped as the die was cast. She could do nothing but follow instructions. For national security, she had no choice but to comply.

"She's a fool to have memorized those names."

"She would have been a fool not to," Darwin countered. "If she lost the paper or if it were discovered, her biggest take ever would have slipped through her fingers. We've verified that the men who broke into her place are tied to the buyer and were likely trying to pilfer the information rather than pay fair and square. We witnessed a big blowup when they returned to him empty-handed."

"So why haven't they made a move yet toward Gloria, then?"

Darwin sighed. "They like pissing me off."

Domino grinned. "That would require emotions. You have none."

"False, Agent Black. Right now I'm dealing with a serious case of impatience. I want the information retrieved and Gloria Brasco stopped before the exchange can be completed, but The Committee wants the buyer caught in the act. Which means we have to wait before we wrap this up. Where is she now?"

Domino glanced up at the ceiling. Probably because Domino resided in the apartment next to hers, Gloria hadn't returned to her own place since the scene in Luke's apartment. Or perhaps, she was terrified that the guys who'd broken in would return and try to beat the information out of her. She'd holed up in Luke's place for the past two nights and since Domino liked having Luke asleep next to her in her bed, she hadn't complained. Besides, she had Luke's place entirely wired. She'd kept a close eye on the woman. So far, she'd done little more than watch game shows and drink inordinate amounts of iced tea while rooting through Luke's sad store of unhealthy snacks.

"Still in Luke's place, but I'll need to verify."

"Could the hard copy list of agents be there with her?"

"I searched the entire apartment thoroughly, but I suppose she could have it on her."

"And the rest of the club?"

"This place is full of nooks and crannies."

"Our techs completely broke down the hard drive information you provided. Nothing is there."

Of course not. That would have been too easy.

"Marcus can't warn his mother?"

"Negative. Even his attorney thinks he's in solitary for fighting."

Domino slid out of bed. Somehow, languishing between her sex-scented sheets while discussing the termination of her lover's stepmother didn't seem right. "I'll keep an eye on Gloria, but she may not make a move for her stash until the buyer contacts her. Any chance we can impersonate him? Speed things up?"

"That is being considered by the strategic team. I'll give you the heads-up when the plan is in place."

"How much time do I have?"

Darwin paused. "We can't imagine that this will go on much longer. Could be as soon as today."

Domino disconnected the call and with a growl, threw her cell phone onto the pillow. Damn it all. Damn it all to hell. She wanted more time with Luke! She'd devoted fifteen years to the protection of her country. She'd given The Shadow her adolescence, her innocence, her heart and soul. She'd never asked for anything in return except for the big fat paycheck they could easily afford and a strong team to watch her back. Now, all she wanted was Luke—something even the all-powerful Committee could not bestow. She'd simply have to find a way to be satisfied with her old life again. Isolated. Disconnected. Alone.

Or perhaps, she was ready for a change? Was that even possible? Just the fact that she knew of the existence of The Shadow made her too valuable to release. She'd heard the words years ago, when she'd been too young to understand.

Once you're in, you're in. There's no turning back.

Back then, she'd had no idea what such an edict would mean. Hell, before she'd met Luke, she hadn't fully realized. Now she felt the entrapment keenly, to the point where she wanted to scream.

But she couldn't think about her own loss now. Not until this case was complete, the mission accomplished. The lives of too many Shadow operatives in too many crucial operations were at stake. If she risked those missions, she risked the safety of every citizen of the United States. She wasn't fooling herself or buying into propaganda. She'd seen the cruelty and hatred of terrorists herself. She knew the stakes and under no circumstances could she elevate her personal needs above those of her country.

Damn it.

She showered and dressed. Neither the scalding hot water nor the ultrasoft fleece workout suit softened her mood. She checked her laptop, now stored permanently in the locked closet in case Luke dropped by, and verified that Gloria was still vegging out on Luke's sofa, depleting his entire stock of Captain Crunch and according to the empty bottles beside her, tequila, though surprisingly, not at the same time. After calling in a backup agent who would watch the building and monitor Gloria's movements from a surveillance vehicle now permanently parked across the street, Domino headed out for some fresh air, using the back stairwell to avoid meeting up with Luke or any of his staff from the club. Her time until execution was slipping away. She needed a workout. Something to stretch out her muscles, to remind her instincts what her life was really about. Nothing could clear her brain with the same quick sweep as a raging case of endorphins.

Domino's hope for a quick getaway vanished the minute she stepped outside the building. She hadn't taken more than three steps into the back alley when she heard gut-wrenching, distinctly feminine sobs from behind a stack of crates.

Domino froze, assessing whether or not she could escape without being seen. She didn't have the chance to execute a successful getaway when Sienna emerged from behind the wooden stacks, a fistful of tissues in one hand and a smoked-out cigarette in the other.

"Oh, great. Just the bitch I wanted to see."

Domino remained quiet, responding only with an arched brow.

"You're probably loving this, aren't you?" She threw her cigarette butt to the ground and stomped it viciously.

"Okay, I'll bite," Domino said, crossing her arms. "What exactly will I love?"

"Mikey dumped me."

The odors from the alley lifted in a noxious miasma to Domino's nose. She'd smelled worse, but in this case, she was sticking around by choice. And she wasn't sure why.

"Don't you have to be involved with a man first before you get dumped?"

"Shut up! You know what I mean."

Did she? What exactly would Luke call it when she disappeared? When she left him alone to deal with the death of his stepmother, at her hand?

"A quick assessment tells me Mikey fucked you and then told you to get lost," Domino concluded. "You expected a different outcome?"

Sienna opened her mouth, but didn't reply. Maybe the twit was actually clueing in to where she went wrong. No one, except for someone clearly delusional, could have anticipated any other ending for Mikey and Sienna than a quickie in some darkened corner, followed by deep regret on the part of the married bouncer and a painful brush-off for the lovestruck waitress. Just like Domino couldn't expect anything other than the most likely outcome for her and Luke.

A broken heart for him. And for her? A lifetime of something she'd never experienced before until him—regret.

"For the record," Domino added. "I don't love what happened to you. I'd have to care one way or another about you in order to enjoy your humiliation, and frankly, I don't. But I don't hate you."

Sienna scoffed, her laugh humorless as she scrambled into her pocket for another cigarette, which she lit with a match struck off the side of the building. "Every woman I meet hates me."

"Maybe because you're a predator."

Sienna's mouth dropped open. Clearly no one to date had had the balls to call this woman what she was.

"What is that supposed to mean?"

"Does predator have too many syllables for you?" Domino asked. "You're a bloodthirsty hunter. You want what isn't yours to take and you're shameless in going after it."

Sienna puffed violently, gesticulating so that the ashes from her cigarette flew in Domino's direction. "So? I'm a woman who knows what she wants. What's wrong with that?"

Domino waved the cinders away. "Ordinarily, nothing. I've lived my life in much the same way for more years than I care to count. But don't be so shocked when other women don't want to have anything to do with you or when a guy screws your brains out and then dumps you on the doorstep. You wanted Mikey. You got him. You didn't expect to keep him because you had sex with him, did you? He has sex with his wife…or did you think she was pregnant via Immaculate Conception?"

Sienna looked away, but not before Domino caught

the lost look that darkened the girl's gaze. Suddenly the irony of her speech struck her. She was giving advice on men? On the insignificance of sex in a relationship? Isn't that really all she and Luke had had, since every other aspect of their interactions had been based on lies? Up until very recently, she'd been prepared to kill him if the order came through. She would have hated doing the job, and she might never have recovered from the act of taking the life of a man she'd come to care about, but she still would have completed her mission. How could she not if he'd been the source of information that risked national security? For fifteen years, the protection of her nation's interests had been her first and only priority. Her actions, along with other Shadow operations, had secretly and anonymously saved thousands of lives all over the world.

Then she'd met Luke. A simple man trying to make a go at a business that was not half as glamorous as most people believed. He worked hard. He used his imagination. He lived his dream, despite the family legacy of larceny and failure. And last night, she'd done with him something she'd never done before—she'd opened her heart. In the midst of their lovemaking, she'd allowed herself to feel emotions she'd previously banished behind the walls she'd erected. Under Darwin's guidance, she'd learned that personal feelings and emotions could cost her a mission, and ultimately, her life. Even in the affairs she'd had in between assignments, she'd known that attaching herself in any way to a man could put more than hearts at risk.

But last night, she'd also acknowledged that she

hadn't chosen her job. She'd been tapped when she was too young to understand the long-range significance of her decisions. She'd been seduced by the excitement of the organization and by the importance of her role in the secret operations that kept her nation safe. She'd been a child with no family, no future, nothing but a girl's fancy daydreams of 007 and *Mission Impossible.*

She stepped aside as memories flooded back— memories she hadn't allowed into her consciousness in years. Hours in front of the television or reading Ian Fleming books while her mother locked herself in her room with her booze and her pills and her all-too-real demons. Afternoons ditching school in favor of the video arcade, where she could feed quarters, stolen from the laundry room in her apartment complex, into the high-tech machines, paying her way into fantasy worlds where her skill with a gun and ingenuity freed her from a life of mundane cruelty. Days at school, tearing through her textbooks in the first few weeks of the semester only to zone out while the other kids tried to catch up. She could see how she'd been an easy target for the sources who'd recruited her, just as Sienna had been an easy lay for Mikey.

She didn't know Mikey well, but she knew the type. Released from the military likely before he'd been ready, trying desperately to find adventure and excitement in the most mundane of careers. Probably loved his wife, too, but like most of the male species, had been unprepared for the emotional roller coaster that marriage promised, especially when kidlets were thrown into the mix. Domino hadn't been surprised when he'd finally caved into Sienna's constant barrage of sexual promises. She was, however, shocked that he'd cast her off so quickly.

Determining that her conversation with the girl had been over for quite some time, Domino moved to leave. She'd advanced ten steps when Sienna called out loudly, "I guess you think I'm a slut, don't you?"

Domino stopped, then figured the girl had to be beyond desperate for someone to talk to if she kept engaging her in conversation.

"I don't judge other women by their sexual choices," she replied.

"What do you judge them by?"

Domino stopped to think. Prior to this mission, judging people, evaluating them, had not been her job. She adhered to a more "live and let live" philosophy that allowed her to do as she pleased without worrying about what other people thought of her and vice versa.

"I try not to judge anyone but myself."

Sienna scoffed. "Oh, so I guess you think you're perfect then."

Domino couldn't even muster up a sardonic laugh. "Not by a long shot, babe. Not by a long shot."

SHE'D RUN SO HARD that she could hardly catch her breath as she jogged back through the alley. Sienna was long gone. The sun was setting over the city and only after Domino dashed up the back stairs and slammed herself into her room did she finally acknowledge the buzzing in her ear.

"Black here," she said, pressing the phone she'd clipped to her waistband.

"The buyer's on the move."

She glanced at the clock. "The club doesn't open for another hour."

"He's either coming in early or trying to throw us off, not knowing we have an agent inserted at his final destination."

"Gloria?"

"We're tapped into the surveillance devices. She's still in Luke's room, but her cell phone received a text message five minutes ago."

"What did it say?"

"Nothing but numbers."

"Code?"

"Negative. Bank account."

"Wire transfer," Domino guessed.

"We're verifying now and so is Gloria. She's headed downstairs to the computer where I'm guessing she can access her offshore accounts, which thanks to her hacker son, she no doubt possesses. Once the money clears, the drop will go down."

Domino headed for the bathroom and turned up the shower to full blast. She barely had any time to clean up, but after her rigorous run, she couldn't blend in to the prearranged plan while wet and sweaty.

"And the list? Has she revealed its location?"

"Not that we witnessed. We'll keep her under supervision while you prepare. You know the drill."

Domino threw the phone onto the bed, peeled out of her sweaty clothes and tore into the shower. The plan they'd cooked up after her tête à tête with Sienna could hardly be considered a drill. Drills required no thought, just practiced motion. Drills considered each and every contingency. This operation tonight would be a bit more along the lines of flying by the seat of her pants.

Nothing about this mission had been by the book. Why start now?

13

FROM THE CORNER of the bar, Luke watched the crowd swell as the disc jockey spun a Rockabilly remix that had the dancers swinging as if they'd been transported back in time. It was gangster theme night, the post popular Club Cicero hosted. Even he looked the part in his black, pin-striped suit with the blood-red satin shirt and spats. He'd learned long ago to embrace the atmosphere because when he did, the paying customers seemed to have a better time.

The waitresses wore black miniskirts with slim silver stripes, fishnet hose, lacy garters, stiletto shoes they'd be bitching about in ten minutes and white satin blouses, most of them unbuttoned to nearly their navels. The bouncers, excluding Mikey, who had not returned to work since his tantrum the day before, were dressed like Luke, but their shirts were black and they wore snap-brim fedoras that conjured images of Al Capone and the St. Valentine's massacre. Oddly enough, security rarely had problems on gangster night. Funny how the idea of mobsters kept the customers in line.

Even Gloria seemed oddly subdued tonight. She'd put on her favorite royal-blue flapper dress complete with feathered headband, but while her mouth worked a mile a minute talking to the customers, her eyes seemed wary. They'd had a short conversation on how she was going to pay back the money she'd stolen, but Luke couldn't shake the feeling that she was really just blowing him off. He suspected that despite that they'd lived within close proximity of each other since he was six years old, Gloria was about to bolt. And unless he wanted to formally press charges—which he didn't—there wasn't much he could do to stop her.

His head chef and door host stopped by with a variety of questions, so once Luke finally had time to breathe again, his eyes went immediately to the door to the apartments. Domino had emerged and instantly, his chest constricted. He'd brought her the costume from the club's store, but he hadn't thought she'd actually put it on.

She was a vision in inky emerald-green. The sheer dress sparkled and shimmered, thanks to the bugle beads covering nearly every inch of fabric, which hugged her body, teased the tops of her knees and swayed with a wicked rhythm as she strode toward him. She wore her own spiked heels and a single band of black, bead-encrusted ribbon across her forehead. For the first time, Luke felt as if Club Cicero was a real speakeasy and Domino Black was a scarlet woman about to lead him into deep, dark temptation.

She licked her lips gingerly, careful not to displace the scarlet color she'd painted on them. "Interesting costume choice."

"I thought you'd look delicious in it," he said,

slipping his hand possessively around her waist. "I wasn't wrong."

Their kiss was long and lingering and Luke couldn't help but absorb all the scented heat her body lent his. Memories of their lovemaking rushed back. For the first time since they'd hooked up, their sex had become more than the manifestation of animalistic lust. The hard-edged, mysterious fantasy woman who'd first attracted him had faded into the background, replaced by a flesh and blood woman who could laugh at herself even as she drove him insane with desire. So much was happening in his life, but no matter the pull of his problems with Gloria or the upheaval in his staff with Mikey missing and Sienna sobbing in the back room, he knew he wanted Domino to stay. Here. With him. For a long, long time, if not forever.

Suddenly Domino pulled back. Only a second later, Craig interrupted.

"Boss, we've got a problem in the kitchen. The fryer is on the fritz."

Always something.

"I'll check it out," he said to Craig. "Do the till drop with the new guy, okay?"

"New guy?" Domino asked.

"I had to call the employment agency and get someone in to replace Mikey. Craig's training him. I'll be back in a few. Grab a drink. We're pushing the gin."

Domino smiled, easily keeping the expression on her face light and seductive until Luke disappeared behind the kitchen door.

Probably the last time she'd see him.

Ever.

She pressed her eyes closed and willed away any show of emotion. She'd known this night would come. She'd said her goodbyes last night, if only in her own heart and mind. Retreating into agent mode would ease the torment, but what was once so easy for her now came only after a struggle. Once the mission was complete, once the buyer was apprehended, the list of names retrieved and Gloria eliminated, she'd grieve for the loss of what might have been between the handsome, honest club owner and the exotic female photographer who'd never really existed.

She slid her hand up her neck so that her mouth was closer to the communication device in her watch. "Where's the buyer?"

Darwin's answer was clipped. "At the bar, fourth down from the front. He's wearing—"

"Got him," she said, spotting a dark-haired, dark-skinned man in a nondescript, slightly outdated suit. Her gaze darted through the crowd and each time she spotted someone she'd bet her entire Swiss bank account was one of his accomplices, she also saw a Shadow agent not two paces away.

"Stand down, Domino. We're covered. Once the exchange is made, the buyer and his men will leave and we'll be right behind them. When you get the word that the deed is done, eliminate Gloria and meet at the rendezvous."

Domino swallowed thickly. "Understood."

She moved quickly through the crowd and positioned herself near the end of the bar. Gin flowed in gimlets garnished with lime, along with martini after martini. The crowd kept Gloria and her staff hopping, but as Domino moved closer, blending behind a large man hogging the end of the bar near the stairwell— Gloria's likely escape route—she saw Luke's step-mother glance left, right, then at the buyer. A nearly imperceptible nod passed between them. Seconds later, Gloria twirled toward the six rows of liquor on shelves behind the bar. Only two rows were low enough to reach. The rest were just for show.

With the help of a stepstool, Gloria reached up and extracted an oddly curved bottle of green liqueur.

Domino's eyes widened. "Is that absinthe?"

Darwin answered. "Zoom in. Yeah, that's the stuff. Damn. It's illegal in the States. No one would serve it."

And from the bottom of the bottle, she untaped a folded sheet of paper.

The list.

Domino tightened her fists.

"Here we go."

The entire transaction took place in seconds. Gloria returned the bottle to its place, tucked the list briefly in the sparkly blue bodice of her dress and climbed down to mix a very dry martini. She chatted, smiled and laughed as she worked, as if the information she'd stuffed next to her heart wouldn't mean the death of at least a dozen Americans who'd risked everything to keep their country safe. She grabbed a cocktail napkin and in a smooth move worthy of a magician's hands, slipped the list into the folds of the absorbent paper. Seconds later, she slid the drink on top of the napkin, pushed the cocktail in front of the buyer, winked and said, "Have this on the house."

Domino seethed, but she held steady. They were almost there.

Out of the corner of her eye, she saw Luke emerge from the kitchen, deep in conversation with one of his waitresses. God, why couldn't he have simply stayed out of the way? She hadn't wanted to see him again. Coward that she now knew she was, she's simply wanted to follow Gloria upstairs, do her duty and then slink away.

She shifted her position, moving in closer. Before she could get the buyer fully in her sights again, he spun around, spotted a Shadow agent and shouted to Gloria, "We've been made!"

A SCREAM. Then two. Then a third. Customers at the bar threw themselves to the ground while others instantly tussled as if a fight had broken out. Men in suits. Women in high heels. Luke rushed forward to try to stop the melee when Gloria pulled a gun from underneath the bar and aimed at a customer with dark hair and skin.

"You idiot! They followed you!"

Luke screamed her name. Or at least, he meant to. He wasn't sure if the desperate sound issuing from his gut formed the word, "Gloria!" or was just a horrified scream. Blood burst on the mirror behind the bar and both his stepmother, and the customer, crumpled to the floor.

Only then did he realize he'd heard a gunshot. No, two shots, reverberating against the glasses that shattered as Gloria fell.

The place went silent. Even the music died. Perhaps Luke could no longer hear it. The floor writhed with whimpering bodies of partiers trying to escape the violence. He nearly tripped as he pushed closer. The only person still standing—the only one he saw—was Domino.

With a gun in her hands.

Luke stumbled backward.

Instantaneously, the stillness erupted into chaos. The dark-haired man with blood oozing from his shoulder was dragged away, quickly spirited out the front doors by men and women dressed in their Club Cicero finest. Customers who'd ducked from the violence before now stampeded toward the back doors, jamming their bodies into the kitchen and out into the alleys. He heard his security guards shouting instructions that no one listened to and Luke knew he should move. Knew he should do something to ensure the safety of his customers, to undo the horrific scene he'd just witnessed, but he couldn't believe what he'd seen enough to act.

Gloria had shot a customer?

Domino had killed Gloria?

When the place was nearly empty, she turned around. Slowly. He could no longer see the gun she'd used. Had it all been a waking nightmare?

Her face, so full of life and sensual promise just a few minutes before, was now frozen like cold steel.

"She tried to kill that man," she explained.

Yes, he'd seen that. He shook his head, not knowing why. Not caring why.

"You shot her," he replied.

"I had to."

Sirens rent the air from the open doors leading to the outside. Luke noticed that Domino didn't move. Didn't try to run or hide.

"They'll arrest you," he said.

She nodded. "I'm sorry, Luke. I really am."

Luke took two shaky steps forward, but couldn't bear to touch even the outer limits of her personal space. He darted left, desperate to get behind the bar, to Gloria. She needed his help. She was dying.

Domino grabbed his arm, held him steady with more force than any woman should be able to manage.

"Don't," she warned him. "She's dead."

"You don't know that!"

Her eyes narrowed and her voice held the same clipped precision as her shot. "Yes, I do."

He stared at her for a long minute. Wondering what she'd just said. Wondering what she'd meant. Wondering who the hell she was.

"She's my mother," he explained in the fewest words he could find. She deserved no real explanation.

"She's a traitor."

"A what?"

"A traitor. That man she almost killed was here to buy the names of undercover agents overseas, names Gloria obtained from your half brother, Marcus."

"Marcus?" As he spoke the name, his heart slammed against his chest. Good God. Marcus, too?

"He's in custody, but he's alive."

The sirens screamed in the air, then went silent.

Domino glanced aside for a second, seeming to listen to something Luke couldn't hear. He leaned forward and for the first time, noticed a tiny device tucked into her ear.

"Come with me," she ordered.

He recoiled, grabbing the bar. He had to stay with Gloria. He had to see. God, he didn't want to see her. He closed his eyes tight and tried to block out the bloody images coursing through his mind, visions spewing from the darkest depths of his nightmares.

Domino slid her hand onto his arm and for a split second, the cold, cruel mask she wore on her face melted away. In her eyes, he saw a flash of the woman he'd made love to so passionately the night before. The woman who'd told him she loved him. The woman he thought he might, with time, love back.

"Please, Luke. Come with me and I'll tell you what I can."

He didn't remember following her. He didn't remember walking up the stairs or unlocking the stairwell or sliding onto the cool leather couch in his living room. The first sound that registered was his cell phone trilling incessantly in his pocket. He lifted the device and looked at it, not certain what to do. Domino gingerly took the mechanism away and shut off the power.

Luke took a deep breath and placed all his focus on answering one question—what had happened?

"Are you a cop?"

Domino recognized the moment Luke regained his control. His voice was level, strong, courageous. It hadn't taken him long to rebound, really, which she told herself was a good sign. She wasn't surprised. He possessed a strength she'd remember long after he'd forced the memory of her out of his mind forever. The conversation they had to have now wouldn't be pretty, but at least, she figured, the matter would be permanently closed.

"Not exactly," she replied, taking advantage of Darwin's edict, just whispered into her earpiece, that she explain the situation as best she could to Luke until agents more skilled at diplomacy could arrive at the scene. The killing of Gloria Brasco was not supposed to have happened in full view of anyone, least of all her stepson.

"Then…what…exactly?"

With each word, his volume rose, his anger escalated, his hatred blossomed like blood from a wound.

"I can't tell you…exactly."

He swallowed hard and the act did ugly things to his jaw. "Why, because then you'd have to kill me?"

He meant no joke, which was fine since never in her life had Domino made light of her occupation. "Maybe. But if I did kill you, I'd simply be doing my job."

Domino ticked off the seconds as Luke's face skewed from confusion to revulsion. "You're not a cop, but you came here to do what? Surveillance on Gloria?"

"Not at first. I was ordered to pursue another target."

"Me?"

She gave a curt nod.

"God, why?"

Darwin's voice buzzed in Domino's ear again and for the first time in years, she had trouble focusing in on what he was saying. She lifted her hand to her ear and concentrated. Something about telling him whatever she felt he needed to know. About signing out. About five minutes.

"Is someone listening?" Luke said, shooting to his feet and staring around his apartment. He'd never find the surveillance devices she'd planted around his private domain. Soon, they'd be gone. Just like her.

"Not for the moment," she replied, removing the sophisticated listening apparatus from her ear canal. Darwin had given her five minutes to say what she felt she had to. The wiretaps would experience a brief enough period of dead air for her to close this chapter of her life forever.

"But they have been? This whole time? Every time we…someone was watching?" He spun around the room, shouting. "Hope you got your jollies, you fucking perverts! Hope you liked watching your government whore suck my dick all in the name of—"

He stopped.

"Why did you trick your way into my bed?"

Domino ignored the spite spewing from his lips. She couldn't blame him for his disillusionment. She had lied. She had tricked her way into his bed. She'd used every talent in her arsenal to insinuate herself as his lover, all the while knowing that the affair wasn't real and wouldn't last.

"Gloria has been selling classified government secrets," she said matter-of-factly. The weight of her revelation forced him back onto the couch. "We have the testimony of your half brother that during his break into the Pentagon computers five years ago, he extracted a file containing the names and locations of deeply imbedded American operatives undercover in the Middle East and Europe. Marcus D'Angelino solicited his mother to sell the names to interested terrorist parties one at a time to finance his restitution payments to the company he embezzled from in order to secure his parole. Gloria was his middleman, his contact on the outside. He gave her the list, along with other important documents, before he went to prison. Once there, he made the acquaintance of an al Quaeda sympathizer doing time for strong-armed robbery. He helped make the connections and Gloria handled the rest. She was paid very handsomely."

Luke shook his head, disbelieving. "If she was making all this money, then why did she steal from me?"

Domino took a deep breath. God, she hated this—spending her last few minutes with Luke running down the situation as if she were at some Agency debriefing—not to mention destroying the memory of a woman who'd been flawed, but whom he loved.

"About six months ago, she and Marcus decided the plot was too dangerous and by releasing each name individually, they were risking getting caught. Ends up they were right. My superiors learned that the information, which directly led to the brutal deaths of a number of undercover operatives, was coming out of this club."

Luke dropped his head into his hands, his elbows balanced precariously on his knees, as if he was too weak from her blows to hold up the full weight of his body. "So they sent you in to find the source and kill her," he said with a sneer.

And she'd followed orders to a T, hadn't she? She'd taken Gloria out with one swift bullet to the brain. But she'd also concluded her business in front of witnesses. Including Luke. She'd acted half out of instinct and half out of duty. Gloria had been armed and while she'd aimed at the terrorist buyer—likely to eliminate the one man who could testify against her and ensure her the death penalty for treason—there had been no telling how many other people the desperate woman would have killed in a mad scramble to escape. Once the buyer told her they'd been made, Gloria had nothing to lose.

But she said none of this to Luke. Though she could hardly remember the loss of her father, or even her mother, so long ago, she did remember not having the capacity to listen to anyone discuss the tragedy until many years later.

She kept her reply simple. "Gloria pulled a weapon. I had no choice."

In a flash, Luke stood. He marched forward until he was inches from her, yet miles away. "This is America, damn it. We always have a choice."

She'd once believed that idealistic sentiment. Once. Maybe. She couldn't remember. All she knew now was that she'd never heard a prettier lie in her entire life.

She took a step back, knowing she could offer no words to comfort him. "That's for my superiors to decide, I suppose."

His eyes narrowed into icy-blue slits. "I hope you lose everything that's important to you."

She closed her eyes and nodded, experiencing only a moment of relief when she heard the Agency facilitators coming up the stairwell. "Trust me, Luke. I already have."

14

One month later

THE REMNANTS OF YELLOW crime tape fluttered on either side of the Closed For Renovation sign someone had taped to the door outside Club Cicero. Luke stared at the streamers, his arms huddling him against the cold that had struck Chicago early this year. His cheeks burned and his eyes stung from the icy autumn wind. Yeah, the wind.

"You're really not reopening?"

Luke glanced over at Mikey, whose big body seemed permanently insulated from the cold. In his arms, he held several packages from the Disney Store and FAO Schwarz. Luke grinned, glad at least that someone had been able to piece their life back together after screwing the wrong woman. Mikey had come clean to his wife, begged her forgiveness, agreed to marriage counseling and now, just a few weeks after the birth of his twin daughters, was still kissing some serious ass. Luke hoped his former security chief made up for his mistakes and, in return, achieved the happiness he deserved. Someone had to.

"I got an offer on the building I couldn't refuse. Almost twice what it's worth."

"You gonna open somewhere else?" The hopeful sound in Mikey's voice cut Luke to the quick. He shook his head, but didn't try to answer out loud.

He'd given up his dream, probably too easily, but somewhere around the time he'd found out his lover was some sort of national security agent, his stepmother was a thief and his half brother was a traitor to his country, he'd lost his love for the business. Club ownership required charm, enthusiasm and finesse. Lately Luke had none of those qualities. He'd become morose, angry and harsh. He decided he simply had to pack up and move. Go somewhere with no memories. Somewhere that would not remind him every minute of the Brasco curse and how low his family had sunk in pursuit of money.

He slapped Mikey on the arm with as much friendliness as he could muster. "You take care of yourself and those babies of yours. And your wife. She's a saint for—"

Mikey nodded hard. "I know. I'm going to spend my whole life making it up to her, but you know, it's better than a whole life spent alone. I made a wrong choice, boss. Now, I'm going to make only the right ones."

Mikey ducked around to the alley where he'd parked the brand-new minivan he'd purchased for his wife, giving one last wave as he rounded the corner. Luke stood in front of the building that had once been his last legacy from his father, then turned away. Choices. Domino had claimed she'd had no choice but to murder his stepmother once she'd fired her gun. Had she really been left with no choice, or had she simply made a decision he knew he personally could never have lived with?

He shook his head, concentrating on the few things he had left to pack. Then, he was heading out of town to parts unknown. He needed more time to work things through. Or at the very least, to forget.

To forget the sight of Gloria's blood splashing on the walls.

To forget the barrage of questions from special agents with branches of government he'd never heard of.

To forget the spicy scent of Domino's perfume.

Because even though he hated her with every fiber of his being, he hadn't managed to forget one single thing about her. And he wouldn't, so long as he stayed in town.

Shoving his hands into his pockets, he walked to Michigan Avenue, where the crowds were subdued early on a Sunday morning. A small line had already formed outside Garrett's Popcorn, compared to the large line in the Starbucks next door. Luke headed toward the train station where he would pick up the orange line out to Ashland. Once there, he'd buy the car he needed to get out of town. He was only half-surprised when a police car pulled up to the curb beside him.

"Mr. Brasco?" the uniformed officer said from his passenger-side window.

Luke stopped, his hackles raised. "Can I help you, Officer?"

The cruiser came to a halt and the cop got out. "We just stopped by your club. Your former bouncer said you were headed to pick up the orange line. Gave us your description. We need your help."

"What's this about?" Luke asked. The matter with Gloria and Marcus had been settled and so far as Luke knew, the local police department had barely been involved.

"We've got a Jane Doe in the hospital. Bad car wreck. Head injury. Can't remember a thing. We've been trying to figure out who she is, but the only thing of use in her purse was this."

He handed Luke a matchbook with the Club Cicero logo on the flap. "We know it's a long shot, especially since you've closed your establishment, but on the off chance she was one of your regulars or maybe an employee, do you think you could come with us and see if you can identify her?"

Luke wanted to say no, but Sienna hadn't been seen or heard from since Mikey had dumped her and Luke had an odd feeling his errant waitress might have ended up in more trouble than she could handle. There was a lot of that going around Club Cicero. A hell of a lot.

"What does she look like?" he asked.

The officer shrugged. "I haven't seen her. The captain just asked me to track you down."

His conscience wouldn't allow him to make excuses, so with a nod, he climbed into the back of the police car, trying not to think about the irony of how his straight and narrow ways had led him right to this very spot. He knew that Sienna had no family in town and as far as he knew, few friends. He imagined she'd gone on some sort of self-destructive bender after Mikey broke things off with her, but he'd been too wrapped up in his own misfortunes to spare her more than a cursory thought from time to time. Of course, the woman in the hospital could be someone he'd never seen, or had seen in the club but didn't personally know. Either way, he had nothing else to do of pressing importance, other than blow this town and start over again somewhere else.

The hospital was just as he remembered hospitals. Cold. Sterile. Overcrowded and stinky. The car crash victim's room was at the end of a long hall, behind a locked pair of doors he thought might be for psychiatric patients. The cop turned him over to a pretty blond nurse in subdued blue scrubs, who explained that the patient had been in the hospital for two weeks and had woken from a coma just a few days ago with no memory of who she was.

The minute Luke crossed over the threshold into the room, his heart stopped.

Domino.

She was standing at the window, her bandaged forehead pressed against the glass. Her right leg was encased in a stark-white cast and her arm hung in a bright green sling.

"You should be in bed, sweetheart," the nurse fussed, rushing to the window and gently guiding Domino back toward the bed. When she turned, there was a vacant look in her eyes. Not cold or detached like he'd seen that night in his apartment after she'd murdered his stepmother. But lost. Uncertain. Unsure.

Vulnerable?

Luke's heart slammed against his chest and he had to exert all his power to stay rooted near the door.

As the nurse tucked her underneath the sheets, she spared him a glance, barely registering his presence. The nurse admonished her to stay put, then scuttled over to Luke with an expectant look in her eyes.

"So, do you know her?"

Luke didn't know what to say. He knew her alias. He'd never outright asked, but he assumed that Domino Black had not been her real name. He wondered if he still had any of the business cards given to him by the dozens of agents who had debriefed him. Wouldn't they know if one of their associates was missing?

"I've seen her before," Luke verified. "I'm not sure what her name is."

The nurse frowned. "Well, that's more than we've had up until now. Maybe if you talk to her, she'll remember you. The specialist who came in to look at her thinks her amnesia will be permanent, but you never know."

A bell rang from the hallway.

"I've got to get that. Can you stay for a moment?"

Luke didn't want to stay. This was the last person he'd ever wanted to see in his life. But she turned her head slowly. The purple stains surrounding those sapphire-blue almond-shaped eyes added to the defenselessness he couldn't ignore. He nodded and the nurse disappeared, shutting the door behind her.

He stepped closer to the bed, his emotions tearing through his body. Once, briefly, he'd thought he loved her. He'd connected with her in a few short days in a way he'd never connected with another woman in his entire life. But she'd lied to him. She'd killed his stepmother, even if he now knew that she'd acted as any federal agent or officer of the law would have under similar circumstances.

His brother, while still alive, would spend the rest of his life in prison, hacking for the good guys, slave to the whim of the government who could easily try him for treason and send him to death row.

Luke had decided the matter was done. He'd committed to putting his regrets and his disappointments and his disillusionments behind him. And he had. Mostly. Except for Domino.

Because some piece of him, some overly romantic part of him, couldn't forget the torn sound in her voice when she'd told him she'd lost everything that mattered to her. Part of him couldn't help but hope that she'd been referring to him. Now she was staring up at him with eyes that didn't mask a thing. She was frightened. She was alone.

He tried to smile at her, but failed miserably.

"Hi," he said.

She glanced at the bedside table, where a small box sat all alone on the stainless steel countertop. "Could you open that for me?"

He complied, revealing a music box that played a tune he didn't recognize. As the music tinkled in the air, she relaxed into her pillows.

Luke realized he had to say something, so he started again with something easy.

"How are you feeling?"

She glanced quickly at her broken leg, wincing as she shifted in the bed. "I've been better."

"Or at least you think you have," he said, knowing she couldn't remember her life before whatever accident had banged her up so badly.

Her gaze, lost momentarily outside the window, returned to him with full, intense force. "No, I've definitely been better. Like that day at the ballpark. That was probably the best day of my entire life."

As if someone had punched him in the chest, he staggered backward, grabbing the edge of the bed to keep from collapsing. She did remember! She'd lied again.

The night she'd shot Gloria, he hadn't had the clarity of mind to say to her what needed to be said—to ask her the questions he needed to ask. Then, she'd disappeared.

The government types who'd talked to him had been hesitant to acknowledge that Domino Black ever existed. By the time he'd gone into her room, every aspect of her had been erased. Even the sheets off the bed they'd shared had been stripped away.

On some nights, when the abandoned club downstairs had echoed with a peculiar silence that made his ears ache, he'd wondered if her coming into his life had been nothing but a hallucination—part fantasy, part dream…part nightmare.

"You're faking?" he asked.

She moved again and if that was phony pain that skewed her face, then she was the best actress he'd ever known.

"The accident was real. Very real," she added with a groan. "The rest was a brilliant idea cooked up by my handler. Who'd have guessed he wanted to finally give me the choice I'd never had before? He set this whole thing up for me, and then gave me this music box. I'm one hundred percent certain that the agency I worked for is listening in on every conversation in this room, but my handler had the box cooked up with a special feature that, when it's open, will keep them from hearing what we say to one another. The agency can still see me," she said without looking up or around for the surveillance cameras that had certainly been installed, "but I don't think they'll get suspicious that you're here. You knew me before I lost my memory. Makes total sense that you'd come here. If for no other reason than to find out if my brain damage is real."

Luke had to shake his head so all the information would solidify in a way he could understand. Why was he talking to her at all? He hated her. Right?

"Why lure me here?" he asked. "I made it clear how I feel about you the night you shot my stepmother."

"Yes, you did," she replied, and her emotionless voice dipped a little. "How you feel about me doesn't change my circumstances. I just can't quit my job and walk away, Luke. Like they say in the movies, I know too much. But the one friend I do have in the world is risking his own career so that Domino Black is destroyed for good. If I pull off this amnesia thing, I can be a new person with a new name and a new life. As long as The Agency thinks I can't remember all the things I've done, I can live." She glanced down at her hand in her lap. "What kind of life I have remains to be seen."

Luke pressed his lips together tightly. He wouldn't feel sorry for her. He wouldn't allow compassion or understanding or worst of all, the last vestiges of that weird love he'd come to feel for her, burst to the surface. He'd learned his lesson. The hard way.

"I'm sorry if it's painful for you to see me," she continued, her eyes veiled by her thick lashes, "but I'm selfish that way, I guess. I had to see you one last time."

He couldn't control his sneer. "And here I was, thinking you were really hurt. That you didn't even know who you were," he said bitterly.

"I don't," she replied, toying with the edge of her sheet with her good hand. "I don't think I ever really have."

She waited for him to stop her. When he didn't, she took a deep breath and continued. "I was recruited into the business at fifteen. I didn't lie to you about my past. My father died. My mother was in a mental institution and died a few years later. I was on the way to big trouble when I was taken in and trained as an assassin. I've been all over the world and I've killed more people than you've probably served in one night at the club. But never in all those years did I ever once want anything more than what The Agency gave me. I don't think I ever knew to want more. Until I met you."

Luke pushed away, shaking the bed so that she braced herself. He'd listened long enough. He didn't want to hear more. He couldn't. Feelings he'd buried beneath layers of anger and betrayal threatened to break free and he couldn't handle it. Not now. Not ever.

"I have to go," he said, charging toward the door.

"I understand," she replied.

He didn't know if it was the catch in her voice or the complete resignation in her raspy tone, but something made him stop and spin toward her.

"How can you possibly understand? Have you ever fallen in love with someone, completely and totally in a few short days and then found out they weren't who you thought they were at all?"

She put the music box gingerly onto her lap. "No, I haven't. When I fell completely and totally in love in a few short days, I found out *I* wasn't who I thought I was at all. Definitely not the same experience."

With a challenging stare, she shut the box. From this point on, Luke knew whatever he said would be heard by the same listening devices that had invaded his own home from top to bottom for God knew how long. If he said the wrong thing now, he had no doubt she'd be eliminated somehow, either locked into her job for the rest of her life or perhaps even killed.

Without this ruse, Domino would never be free to live her life on her own terms. Literally they owned her. And if her so-called handler had come up with this brilliantly simple plan to ensure her freedom, who was he to argue?

He grabbed the doorknob.

Who was he?

The man who loved her.

He spun around, stalked to the bed and yanked the music box out of her hands. This time when it opened, the tinkling tune made sense.

"Take Me Out to the Ball Game."

A lob of something big and thick and impregnable lodged in his throat. He figured it was a mixture of fear, pride and longing. He and Domino had really never had a chance, had they? She'd come into his life with a nefarious ulterior motive, but one that no longer factored into the decisions they made now. She could be free. And without Gloria and Marcus and the building and his devotion to making the club a success, in a sense, he was free, too.

"I'm terrified," he admitted.

Her grin was tentative, as if she, too, shared his fear. "I'd think you a fool if you weren't."

"How can I trust you?"

She shook her head. "I have nothing to lose anymore, Luke. Nothing except you. And if I lose you, I'll be left with the sum total of all I've accumulated in my lifetime—nothing. No friends, except my handler, who I'll never be able to speak with again. No relationships. Nothing but a whole mess of emotional angst and the love I feel for you."

Luke sat on the bed beside her, careful not to disturb her broken leg. "Seems like a hundred years ago since I loved you, and yet…I don't think I've ever considered doing anything as risky as loving you again."

Her smile was tiny. Almost shy. Almost. "I've lived a rather risky life until now and I've done okay. I met you, didn't I? I consider that better than okay."

Like the night they made love in her room for the first time, their kiss was soft, tentative and exploratory. Luke accepted that despite her job, despite her actions, despite everything that scared the living shit out of him, she tasted the same. His fingers found the flesh on her cheeks and neck as familiar as always. As perfectly matched to his as he'd dreamed. When she sighed softly, he knew he couldn't let her go.

He pulled back. "How will we pull it off?"

Her eyelashes fluttered over blue eyes dark with passion. Not just lust, like when they first met, but the kind of desire that was created when a man and a woman fell in love.

"Thanks to my handler, the doctors will insist my brain damage is permanent. You'll agree to take custody of me as the only person who knows who I am. You'll probably be visited soon after by government types and you'll have to convince them that you see my amnesia as a chance to win back the woman you once loved. For us to have a life after all we've lost."

"How do we know they'll believe us?"

"We don't. But my handler and I are betting that after a while, they'll simply want to put this entire matter to rest. Then, we'll have to really start over. Never discuss the past. Look only ahead to the future. I love you, Luke." She let out a pent-up breath. "I never thought I'd get a chance to say those words to you again."

Luke took a deep breath. This wouldn't be easy. But then, who ever said love was easy?

"I promise to give you lots of opportunities to say those words from now on. I love you, too."

He snuggled closer and stared into her eyes, which seemed to glitter with tears she was fighting to control.

Putting the past behind him was something he should have done a long time ago. The idea of starting fresh, with new names and a new location, gave him the kind of rush he'd felt when his fantasy woman had first slipped in his nightclub and turned his life upside down. With the negative, destructive forces now gone from his life, all he had left was the future that lay before him, which could be either a lifetime of bitterness or a lifetime of love. Luke had a choice.

Their kiss this time was neither soft nor tentative, but brimming with a thousand possibilities, each one more exciting than the next. That was the effect Domino had had on him when they'd first met and that was the effect she still had on him now. Most importantly, that was the effect that would keep their love going now and forever.

* * * * *

"OH, NO!"

The reaction slipped out before Emma Valentine could stop it, for there stood the very man she most wanted to avoid seeing again.

He didn't look any happier to see her.

"Well, come on, get on board," he said gruffly. "I won't bite." One eyebrow rose. "Though I might nibble a little," he added, mostly to amuse himself.

But she wasn't paying any attention to what he was saying. She was staring at him, taking in the royal blue uniform he was wearing, with gold braid and glistening badges decorating the sleeves, epaulettes and an upright collar. Ribbons and medals covered the breast of the short, fitted jacket. A gold-encrusted sabre hung at his side. And suddenly it was clear to her who this man really was.

She gulped wordlessly. Reaching out, he took her elbow and pulled her aboard. The doors slid closed. And finally she found her tongue.

"You…you're the prince."

He nodded, barely glancing at her. "Yes. Of course,"

She raised a hand and covered her mouth for a moment. "I should have known."

"Of course you should have. I don't know why you didn't." He punched the ground-floor button to get the elevator moving again, then turned to look down at her. "A relatively bright five-year-old child would have tumbled to the truth right away."

Her shock faded as her indignation at his tone asserted itself. He might be the prince, but he was still just as annoying as he had been earlier that day.

"A relatively bright five-year-old child without a bump on the head from a badly thrown water polo ball, maybe," she said defensively. She wasn't feeling woozy any longer and she wasn't about to let him bully her, no matter how royal he was. "I was unconscious half the time."

"And just clueless the other half, I guess," he said, looking bemused.

The arrogance of the man was really galling.

"I suppose you think your 'royalness' is so obvious it sort of shimmers around you for all to see?" she challenged. "Or better yet, oozes from your pores like…like sweat on a hot day?"

"Something like that," he acknowledged calmly. "Most people tumble to it pretty quickly. In fact, it's hard to hide even when I want to avoid dealing with it."

"Poor baby," she said, still resenting his manner. "I guess that works better with injured people who are half asleep." Looking at him, she felt a strange emotion she couldn't identify. It was as though she wanted to prove something to him, but she wasn't sure what. "And anyway, you know you did your best to fool me," she added.

His brows knit together as though he really didn't know what she was talking about. "I didn't do a thing."

"You told me your name was Monty."

"It is." He shrugged. "I have a lot of names. Some of them are too rude to be spoken to my face, I'm sure." He glanced at her sideways, his hand on the hilt of his sabre. "Perhaps you're contemplating one of those right now."

You bet I am.

That was what she would like to say. But it suddenly occurred to her that she was supposed to be working for this man. If she wanted to keep the job of coronation chef, maybe she'd better keep her opinions to herself. So she clamped her mouth shut, took a deep breath and looked away, trying hard to calm down.

The elevator ground to a halt and the doors slid open laboriously. She moved to step forward, hoping to make her escape, but his hand shot out again and caught her elbow.

"Wait a minute. *You're* a woman," he said, as though that thought had just presented itself to him.

"That's a rare ability for insight you have there, Your Highness," she snapped before she could stop herself. And then she winced. She was going to have to do better than that if she was going to keep this relationship on an even keel.

But he was ignoring her dig. Nodding, he stared at her with a speculative gleam in his golden eyes. "I've been looking for a woman, but you'll do."

She blanched, stiffening. "I'll do for what?"

He made a head gesture in a direction she knew was

opposite of where she was going and his grip tightened on her elbow.

"Come with me," he said abruptly, making it an order.

She dug in her heels, thinking fast. She didn't much like orders. "Wait! I can't. I have to get to the kitchen."

"Not yet. I need you."

"You what?" Her breathless gasp of surprise was soft, but she knew he'd heard it.

"I need you," he said firmly. "Oh, don't look so shocked. I'm not planning to throw you into the hay and have my way with you. I need you for something a bit more mundane than that."

She felt color rushing into her cheeks and she silently begged it to stop. Here she was, formless and stodgy in her chef's whites. No makeup, no stiletto heels. Hardly the picture of the femmes fatales he was undoubtedly used to. The likelihood that he would have any carnal interest in her was remote at best. To have him think she was hysterically defending her virtue was humiliating.

"Well, what if I don't want to go with you?" she said in hopes of deflecting his attention from her blush.

"Too bad."

"What?"

Amusement sparkled in his eyes. He was certainly enjoying this. And that only made her more determined to resist him.

"I'm the prince, remember? And we're in the castle. My orders take precedence. It's that old pesky divine rights thing."

Her jaw jutted out. Despite her embarrassment, she couldn't let that pass.

"Over my free will? Never!"

Exasperation filled his face.

"Hey, call out the historians. Someone will write a book about you and your courageous principles." His eyes glittered sardonically. "But in the meantime, Emma Valentine, you're coming with me."

SAVE UP TO $30! SIGN UP TODAY!

INSIDE *Romance*

The complete guide to your favorite Harlequin®, Silhouette® and Love Inspired® books.

✓ Newsletter ABSOLUTELY FREE! No purchase necessary.

✓ Valuable coupons for future purchases of Harlequin, Silhouette and Love Inspired books in every issue!

✓ Special excerpts & previews in each issue. Learn about all the hottest titles before they arrive in stores.

✓ No hassle—mailed directly to your door!

✓ Comes complete with a handy shopping checklist so you won't miss out on any titles.

SIGN ME UP TO RECEIVE INSIDE ROMANCE ABSOLUTELY FREE

(Please print clearly)

Name

Address

City/Town   State/Province   Zip/Postal Code

(098 KKM EJL9)

Please mail this form to:
In the U.S.A.: Inside Romance, P.O. Box 9057, Buffalo, NY 14269-9057
In Canada: Inside Romance, P.O. Box 622, Fort Erie, ON L2A 5X3
OR visit http://www.eHarlequin.com/insideromance

IRNBPA06R   ® and ™ are trademarks owned and used by the trademark owner and/or its licensee.

If you enjoyed what you just read,
then we've got an offer you can't resist!

Take 2 bestselling
love stories FREE!
Plus get a FREE surprise gift!

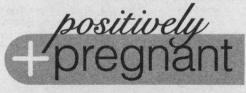

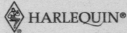